Is He
All That?

A Novel

Bianca Moore

DEDICATION

This book is dedicated in loving memory of my grandparents:
Anna Stanley, Leroy David Wilson, and Esther Mae Wilson.
You will never be forgotten. I miss you all so much.
I love you always,
Tysha

ACKNOWLEDGMENTS

First, I would like to give all thanks, honor and glory to my Lord and personal savior Jesus Christ. He made me realize I had a true talent for writing at a very young age.

To my son, Xeondre', whom I love with all my heart. Some nights, you would come into the family room and say "Mom, are you still working on your book, it's getting late?"

To my mother, Gloria Berry, father, Orvillee Banks, stepmother, Vickie Banks, and stepfather, Henry Berry, for always being there for me. To Granpop ("Pops"). You always say, "Get on the road before it gets dark" and I never do. To my brother, Corey Sharp, and sister-in-law, Yvonne Sharp ("Sis"). I love you guys. To my little sister, Rah'Kera. I know you will do well in college. You can do it! To my godmother, Francine, who got me hooked on the *Young and the Restless* at a very young age. To my best friend, Shemeka Smith, for ALWAYS being there for me. I love you like a sister. To Duane Smith Sr., for always keeping me laughing. You are a crazy man! To Mrs. Judith Howell, my English teacher at Cambridge South Dorchester High School. To Dr. Daryl Dechaby, my English professor in college. To Dr. Abdul Shaikh, my advisor in graduate school. To my stylist, LaShon, in Waldorf, MD for always keepin' a sista's hair tight. I am the second easiest client that you have. To my other stylist Toni of "Braids by Toni." You used to tell me, "Tysha, please comb your hair before you come in." LOL.

To Yonder, author of *What I Do Is Taboo*, and also known as my play big brother, thanks so much for being a true friend and for being an inspiration to me as well as my writing mentor. Thanks for all the writer tips and guidance and for pushing me to finish this book. Check Yonder out at www.whatidoistaboo. com. To Jessica Tilles for packaging my book and providing me with so much great information about this business. You were a huge help and cleared up a lot of things for me. My godchildren: Rod'Neshia, Deja, Alaizah, and Kambren. God-Mommy loves you all very much. To my brunch crew: Adrienne ("AD"), Tracey ("TLC"), Terri, Ayana, and Cliff. Our brunches at Jasper's could make us millions of dollars. We could have our own reality show because we really sound off about some stuff during brunch, don't we? To "The FAM," you are a crazy bunch of people! It's a blessing how we all met and still keep in touch. Sometimes people don't believe me when I tell them how we all met. To some very special friends that are near and dear to my heart: TaKira. You are a different kind of crazy...ha, ha, ha. We had some fun times in '93 and '94 and you were the first friend I met when I moved to the DC area. Stephanie Brown. Love you like a sister! Marly Machacon ("Machacon"). Thanks for always giving it to me straight. Jay and Willistine Brown (the best realtors around). Check them out at www.brownteam2000. com. You guys are the best realtors! Monica Blyther, Martha Mhlanga. You are a very special friend and always know the right things to say, especially when I start sounding off and turning into "Bianca". LOL. Leslie Britt (my other play big brother).

Thanks for your words of wisdom and for always bringing me back to reality. Damone Best (my play little brother). Thanks for being a real friend. Cheryl Botts (my Mary Kay consultant for life), Jackie, Jay Henson, Marquis Green, Donte' Taylor, Brian Carson (B-Dizzle), Dwayne Alexander, LaSonya, Lisa. The best damn stepmother period! Ladies, take note of this. If you are as lucky as I am to have a stepmother for your child like this woman, then you are truly blessed. To my entire extended family in New Orleans (The Peters family). Shavone, Aaron Cain ("The King" and the best damn photographer period). All my former co-workers at DISA/JITC: You guys are the best. To all my people at JDISS. To my Aunts, Uncles, and cousins. I love you all. To my nieces Tyshauna, Tykia, Shanay, Brooklyn and ZaKera. My nephews Tyler, Shaquille, Javion, Kahlei, Zhaden, Zion, and Ra'Sai, Auntie loves you all! To my favorite cousins, Tyisha, Tynesha, Bell, Dion, Duane Jr., Tykesha, Pete, Deanna & Craig Milligan, Nichelle & Shawn Cook, Bessie & Eugene Stewart. Sherill, Jimmy (RIP), Rolinda, Marti, Tianne, and Tomeka. Also, thanks to Sharon Harper, owner of the Barber Lounge for Men in Waldorf, MD, for being such an inspiration and just a beautiful person. If I forgot anybody, please don't take it personally as it was not intentional. I love you all. Thanks for your support.

Is He All That?

Chapter One

MORNING CHAOS

L ord knows I don't feel like going to work today. Still lying in my bed, I'm wondering if I should call in *slick*! Sounds like a great plan. I could spend my entire day at the spa instead of dealing with those idiots at the office. Working in Washington, DC can really work on my nerves. It is such a congested area. I wake up at 5:00 a.m. just to be out of the door by 6:00 a.m. Some days I drive in, other days, I catch the train. It depends on my mood. Since I'm already in somewhat of a nasty mood, I'll take the Metro.

My alarm clock finally goes off, and I shut it up with a good smack. It's very rare I wake up before that thing goes off. My calling in *slick* idea soon passes, so I pry myself from my comfortable bed and slip into my robe. Usually, I get a cup of coffee, sit on the sofa for fifteen minutes, and watch a bit of the news before I get myself together.

I have a cozy, two-level, two-bedroom condominium I rent in Fort Washington, Maryland. I need to buy a house one of these days. After catching up on what's going on in the world and the weather forecast, I drag myself up to the bathroom and start my daily ritual of getting ready to head to work.

I wash my face, brush my teeth and smile at my brown features in the mirror. I'm thankful my parents could afford braces when I was a teenager. My teeth used to be jacked up! Thank God, they aren't anymore. I'm petite, one hundred twenty pounds soaking wet and I can't stand my hair. It's so curly and hard to manage at times. It's somewhat long right now, but I feel a haircut coming on. In high school, my friends wished they had my naturally curly hair, but I told them they were better off with their perms. I come from a small family—one brother and one sister—I'm the big sister.

I head out the door promptly at 6:00 a.m., drive to the Branch Avenue Metro station, park, and hop on the train. While I'm waiting for the train to leave the station, I pull out some brochures I picked up from a few graduate schools and peruse them. Graduate school has been on my mind lately, but I don't think I'm ready yet. I should be more serious about going before filling out these long and tedious applications.

As the train pulls out of the station, I look up to see a fine brother sitting across from me reading the paper. I can't help but to size him up, looking good in his tan-colored suit, olive-colored shirt with a matching tie and some…wait a minute. Are those cowboy boots? Hmm…those boots do look sexy on him though.

He looks up, gives me a smile, and says, "Good morning."

"Good morning."

The first thing comes to mind is how he's so polite. I bet he has a girlfriend or is married. I glance at his left hand for a wedding band, but I don't see one, not even that telltale wedding band line. He resumes reading his paper and I attempt to stop staring at him by looking out the window at the passing darkness of the underground tunnel, but all I see is his reflection.

I get off the train at Gallery Place. As usual, people are pushing and shoving, and rushing to get to their destinations. I walk in the direction of 9th and F Streets toward my office. I work near the Verizon Center, where my favorite team plays. I love going to the Wizards' games and I am a diehard basketball fan. I can talk trash with the best of them. The men in my office tell me, "You're a woman; you're not supposed to know this much about basketball." I'm constantly getting free tickets from the lawyers in my building. There are three companies occupying this building: a software company, a law firm, and an engineering firm. I work for the software company. We design computer-learning software for children of all ages. We have everything from Science to Math.

I show my badge to the toy cops guarding the building. They call themselves security guards. Except for a few, most of their asses need gym memberships, so whom the hell are they supposed to protect? Shit, I could protect their asses. I smile and greet them, before stepping into the elevator with three women I've never seen before. Most likely, they work for the law firm or the engineering firm. The petite, short, white woman with red hair looks like she just rolled up out of the bed. The Asian woman is having a serious one-on-one with her PDA and not paying any of us any mind. The sister looks like she made it out of the ghetto and trying her best not to show it, but I know her type. She is straight out of the 'hood! At any rate, I say good morning to everyone because that's just the country girl in me. One thing about country people, we speak to everybody.

I press the button for my floor and listen for a response from the women, but there were none. The elevator doors open and they step off the elevator.

In a stern voice, I say, "Y'all bitches heard me speak to you, and you ignored me."

The expressions on their faces are priceless as the elevator doors close. They stand with their mouths open. As I said earlier, I woke up in a stank up mood. It really annoys me when I speak to people, and they don't open their damn mouths. The people I work with know me, so they know better. Half the time, they speak to me first before I even have a chance to say anything.

I get to my desk, log on to my computer and check the pressing emails that I know are waiting for me. I'm one of four business analysts in the office. It's our job to decide the order in which projects are pushed out. We look over new ideas for software from the developers and decide if we should pursue the project now, later or never. There are two of us to an office and it's very spacious. I have an interesting job, and I love it. It's only stressful when I have a deadline to meet, or when I turn down a developer's proposal for a new product. That's when he gets really pissed at me and comes into my office to plead his case.

Most of the time, my girl, Marilyn, is in the office with me, and she'll have my back. Marilyn is a business analyst, too, and we share an office.

"Oh Lord, here comes Ron, Shayla," Marilyn says, heading for her desk. "Are you ready for him?"

I shake my head and moan. Ron is quite a handful, and I am in no mood to deal with him today.

Hurricane Ron blows into our office and slams the door. "Who the hell do you think you are, Shayla Richardson, turning down my software idea? Do you know how much time I put into this shit, and you just toss it to the side like I'm some fuckin' amateur programmer straight outta college?"

I immediately jump up from the sofa, ready to light his ass up like a Christmas tree. "Ron, you need to chill and calm your ass down. Who the hell do you think you are, comin' up in my office, slammin' the door and actin' a damn fool?"

Breathing heavy, he looks at me. He looks like he's about to have an asthma attack. Marilyn is sitting at her desk, looking at Ron. She's having a hard time containing her laughter. I try to contain my laughter, as well.

"I just can't believe you," he protests. "I'm one of the best programmers you've got and this is how you treat me?" He paces the floor, mumbling something under his breath that I can't understand.

I walk over to him. "Ron, first of all, I did not turn down your idea. When I wrote the review for the proposal, I said we were not going to pursue the social studies software idea yet, but at a later date. You obviously didn't read to see what that date was. We will bring your idea on the market in three to four months."

Ron looks at me with evil eyes. "I read your bullshit review, Shayla, and you must think I'm stupid. Three to four months in your world means a year. I've been working with you long enough to read between the lines."

I give him my don't-fuck-with-me-today face and his gay ass sucks his teeth, rolls his eyes at me, and storms out of my office, flinging the door open so hard it hits the wall. People outside are laughing at him, whispering and being nosey. There are also a few onlookers peeping out of their cubicles. They are used to all the actions and live for the daily drama. The other business analysts down the hall encounter the same crap as Marilyn and me, only they are a bit softer than we are. We don't take any crap off the computer geeks or anyone else for that matter.

After having the morning from hell, Marilyn and I decide to walk to Fuddruckers for lunch. As usual, the line is almost out the door. Fuddruckers has the best burgers in DC. We finally make it to the front of the line and order our food. We find a seat and enjoy our lunch.

"I still can't believe that faggot came into our office actin' like that," I say, taking a bite of my burger.

"Neither can I," replies Marilyn. "Ron is a trip; he swears he's a woman with his sweet ass."

We both crack up laughing. I glance over near the counter and see the brother from the train this morning. He's getting his drink and trying to find a place to sit. Dayum, he's even finer standing up. He has nice broad shoulders and sexy toned arms, looking like Mel Jackson from *Soul Food*. You know the one that got his ass kicked by Lem. He notices me and walks toward the table.

"Hello, again," he says in a deep masculine voice, as my eyes are drawn to that nice suit and sexy cowboy boots. He even licks his lips. My hormones can't take this today.

"Hi, nice to see you, again," I say, a tad bit nervous.

Marilyn is really looking confused, so I tell her how we met on the train this morning.

"I'm sorry. I didn't get your name from this morning. I'm Shayla."

"I'm David, and you're cute."

I blush. "Thanks, David. Umm, this is my co-worker Marilyn."

Marilyn extends her hand as she speaks to him. I try not to read too much into that comment he just made. He seems a little forward.

"Can I talk to you outside for a second?" he asks.

"Sure, Marilyn, please excuse me for a minute. I'll be right back."

We go outside and chitchat for a couple minutes.

"So, why is someone as beautiful as you not married?"

Oh Lord, here come the pickup lines. "Hell if I know! The only thing I can think of is I haven't found the right person yet."

"Really, have you even come close?"

"Nah, not really. I haven't been in a relationship in a really long time."

I'm wondering what's up with all the questions, so I throw a few back at him. "So, what's your story? Why aren't you married or involved with anyone?"

"Can I tell you over dinner tonight?"

"Sure."

We exchange numbers and make plans to meet up later on tonight.

He gets his food and I return to the table. Marilyn is anxiously awaiting a report.

"So, did y'all exchange numbers?" she says with excitement in her eyes.

"Yep, and guess what else? We are going to dinner tonight."

"Go 'head, girl. Get your man!"

Marilyn is one crazy chick; very humble, but surprises me at times. She's older than I am, so she has lots of wisdom. Whenever I'm in a jam about something, I ask her for advice because she's always so positive about everything. You won't ever hear any negativity come out of her mouth. We are total opposites. She holds back a lot, and I say whatever the hell is on my mind and don't give a damn. We finish our lunch and head back to the office.

Entering the building, one of the security guards stops me to talk trash about last night's Wizards game.

"What happened to your Wizards last night, Shay?"

"I don't know what happened. I think we just made a couple bad plays, but we're going to make it better tomorrow night.

Matter of fact, I got tickets to tomorrow's game, but I can't make it because I have a deadline to meet. Do you want them?"

He looks at me as if he's a little shocked. "For real? Sure, I'll take 'em."

"Okay, I'll bring them in with me tomorrow. I really wish I could go, but I can't. John Wall is a beast on the court, ain't he? That dude had 40 points last night."

"Hey, thanks Shay, I appreciate it."

"No problem, man. Enjoy the game." I love seeing John Wall play!

I attempt to sort through the rest of the emails and write up reviews and recommendations for projects. I know Hurricane Ron is going to come back in here soon to apologize. He already sent me an email saying he was sorry. He always does. He will apologize via email first, and later apologize in person.

I'm a little curious about David and can't wait to learn more about him. Tonight's dinner should be interesting. I hope it's not another wounded brother not looking for a relationship right now or who just wants to fuck. That seems to be the line of the year with men in this area. "I'm not looking for a relationship" is the only thing I hear lately from these jokers. I don't know what's up with that.

I head home and relax a little until David calls, saying he's made a reservation for six o'clock at the Sakura Japanese Restaurant in Waldorf, and for me to meet him. I've never had Japanese food before. I've had Chinese, Tai, and Korean, but not Japanese.

I jump in the shower to freshen up and pick out a nice pair of jeans, a shirt, a jean jacket, and a pair of black boots. I don't want to be too dressy. It is only dinner, not a black tie affair. I purposely arrive at the restaurant a little late. I never arrive to a date on time. It makes you look too pressed. I notice David from across the room and he sees me, too. He gets up, walks toward me and greets me with a hug. Dayum he smells good. Lookin' all good, clean cut and sexy just like I like 'em.

We sit down and the waiter comes over to take our drink orders. I order a glass of wine and he orders a Long Island Iced Tea.

"You look nice," he says.

"Thank you."

"Have you been here before?"

"Nope, but I've heard of it. They say the food is really good."

We look over our menus a little and I catch him peeking at me. What in the world is he doing?

"So, you want to hear my story, Shayla?"

"Sure, I know it must be interesting."

"Well, that's one way of putting it."

Oh shit, I'm getting nervous. This sounds like it's going to be one hell of a story. Let me brace myself and at least look calm and collected.

He tells me he is a single father and he just got out of a long-term relationship with the mother of his child. His daughter is twelve. She was born when he was only sixteen. I calculate that we're around the same age. He also gives me that line that I knew I was going to hear eventually.

"I'm not looking for a relationship right now," he says. "I just want to focus on being a good father to my daughter and set a good example for her."

I respect this man so much already because he's a single dad, and how many of those do we have out here? Not many. Although, I am very disappointed to hear he's not looking for a girlfriend. He could turn out to be a really good friend, so I'll just go with the flow for now.

"You know," he continues. "When my daughter was born, I was only in the eleventh grade. My parents were pissed when I told them I had gotten somebody pregnant. I was the quarterback of the football team. I was in the honors society and the chess club. I was a superstar nerd!" We both crack up laughing. "I had no idea what I had just gotten myself into. I mean, my parents were both around for my entire upbringing, so I didn't understand at first why I was in this situation. I guess I just got caught up, you know? I knew I should have been using protection, but I was stupid enough to believe she was on the pill. I'm not blaming her. I blame myself. My daughter is here now and I wouldn't have it any other way. Do you have any children, Shayla?"

"No, not yet, but would love to have a few one day, if I get married. If not, I'll just adopt one."

"That's a good plan. I don't want to have any more unless I get married."

Our food arrives and we eat and continue to talk. He tells me how much of a deadbeat parent his daughter's mother is and that's why he decided to raise her. He's had the little girl since she was five years old. I don't know what his daughter's mother did to him, but she really hurt him. He is wounded for sure. He spends most of the evening telling me how much he hates his daughter's mother, which is a real turn off for me. He was doing all right until he started doing that. He is also telling me how much of a handful the little girl is.

"So, why are you by yourself?" he asks me, and so I tell him.

"I'm a woman who has had quite a few games ran on her and who has been stepped on a few times, so that's why I have tough skin. I can spot a game really quick and can tell pretty quickly what someone is after," I say, wanting him to know I knew his little game already, so I thought I would throw him a few hints.

Right now, I'm getting the impression that this is a frustrated single father with a pre-teen at home stressing him the hell out and he just needed to get out of the house. These niggas be killin' me with this shit. I'm actually getting a little pissed off, because if he's not interested in me then why does he want to have dinner with me? Why the fuck are we here? I have yet to figure out the male species; they are so funny.

"I'm almost thirty years old," I continue, "and I'm at a point in my life where I'm looking for a steady relationship with the potential to blossom into something more serious. I'm tired of this dating game. I've been playing it since age eighteen. It's getting really old. I don't like going to clubs because the same dudes are always looking for someone to take home and fuck. I'm not looking for that when I go into a club. I'm not looking for that at all. I go to get my dance on, have a couple drinks and have fun. I remember when I went out with my girl, Kathy, and a few of her friends for her thirtieth birthday at Zanzibar on the waterfront in DC, and we were having such a good time. The drinks were good and the music was off the hook. They were playing all the old songs from back in the day when I was in high school. I'm talking 90s music: Lil' Kim's *Crush on You*, Junior Mafia's *Get Money*, Biggie Smalls' *One More Chance* and Tupac's *I Get Around*. I was gettin' my groove on for real until this horny fool walks up and starts dancing with me and keeps putting his dick up against my ass. I push him back to let him know to back up off me. He backs up for a while then starts up again. I said 'Look muthafucker! Stop trying to fuck me on the dance floor.' I don't think he heard me because he kept on, so I left his dumb ass right there dancing alone. My girls saw the whole thing and they were cracking up laughing. Whatever happened to going out to clubs and having a good time without all the pressure?"

Our date ends around ten, and he says, "I had a really good time and would like to stay in touch with you and go out again." We head out to the parking lot and stand in front of the restaurant.

"Sure, we can go out again anytime, just let me know."

I knew damn well I wasn't going out with his boring stressed out ass again. I usually know after the first date if there will be a second date. I just had to say something so I could get to my car quicker.

He is looking at me as if he wants to kiss me, so I just come out and ask him the obvious question.

"Why are you looking at me like that?"

"I was just wondering if your lips were as sweet as your personality."

"Oh really?"

"Yeah, really," he says, looking me up and down seductively and licking his lips.

I kiss him on the cheek because I don't want to leave the wrong impression by kissing him on the lips on the first date. By the way, he has been looking at me; it is definitely time for me to leave.

He smiles and says, "Good night."

"Good night," I say, walking to my car.

I drive home, get into my PJs and chill for the rest of the evening. Fifteen minutes later, my phone rings and it is David.

"Hi, Shayla. I hope you haven't gone to bed yet."

"Nah, I'm just sitting here watching a little TV."

"I just wanted to call and say that I had a great time, and I hope to see you again soon."

"I had a great time, too, David. Thanks so much for dinner."

"Oh, you are more than welcome." We say our goodbyes and hang up.

I'm sitting on my couch drifting off a little, and the phone rings again. This time it's Marilyn, wanting details about my date.

"It was okay, but not too exciting." I tell her about his daughter and how stressed out he seemed.

She puts a positive spin on it, of course, and says, "Maybe he had a bad day and needed to talk."

"Damn right that dude needed to talk, but I'm no fuckin' psychiatrist! I now feel like I've known him for years."

We both crack up laughing.

"Was he a gentleman though?" she asks.

"Yeah, he was a perfect gentleman, but I did get the impression he was waiting for a kiss from me when the date ended."

"For real, girl?"

"Yeah, he seemed to think he was going to put his tongue down my throat on the first date. Is he crazy?"

"What would you have done? Reject him?"

"Yes, ma'am, I would have rejected him. I'm not like that. He's not looking for a relationship, but he wants to put his tongue in my mouth. Dumb ass!"

"Girl, you are too much."

"Hey, Marilyn, I'll be working from home tomorrow. The cable guy is coming to put the cable jack in my guest room. If anyone needs me, they can call me here."

"Okay, girl, it's getting late. I'll talk to you tomorrow."

Bianca's Thoughts:
Although dating is fun and exciting at times, I can't stand a boring ass man! That dude would never get a second date from me. Although I admire him for being a single father, he really needs to

be sitting on someone's couch getting some therapy. He had quite a lot to talk about on a first date. I think he got a little too personal with Shayla and she certainly took notice of that. Also, it's not a good idea to talk bad about the other parent. For example, if you are the father raising the child, don't talk bad about the mother. The same thing should apply to a woman raising a child without the father. You should never bad mouth the father to anyone, especially a date. What a turnoff that is. It's totally disrespectful to that parent and it certainly doesn't make you look like too good of a person. Regarding him not wanting to be in a relationship right now, okay, that's fine, but did he have to be so blunt about it? He could have smoothed it over by saying, "I don't want to be in a relationship right now, but I am open to dating because you never know what can happen" or something to that effect.

Chapter Two

ALL KINDS OF MEN

Today, I'm working from home and am getting a lot accomplished. I don't have to worry about anyone storming into my office with their complaints and whining about me not approving their idea, or having to deal with anyone else's drama. I am working in my PJs and robe. I figure I'd better make myself look presentable soon, being that the cable guy is coming between eleven and three. Don't you hate when they do that? The cable people, electric company, furniture stores, phone company. They all act as if we don't have a fuckin' life, as if we're home all day or something! I race upstairs and throw on a pair of jeans and one of my many Spelman sweatshirts. It is now noon and no one has yet to show up from the cable company. Ain't this a bitch? All this shit for one cable jack. I attempt to concentrate more on work, but instead I think about all the different types of men I've dated and have tried to run games on me.

Ladies, you know how you first meet a man and on the surface, it looks like he has everything together, or at least that's the way he tries to portray it to be? Then a couple months later, you find out that everything he told you was a damn lie. It's amazing how people send their representatives on a damn date, faking and pretending to be someone else. They are wonderful in the beginning, and then a couple months down the road they turn out to be real assholes. Why can't people just tell the truth?

Here are the top three types of men I continue to run into:

Mr. I'm Not Looking For A Relationship—this dude is a trip right here. He will call you a lot, want to hang out and spend time with you, but the minute you bring up anything closely resembling a date, commitment, or a relationship he disappears! He's ghost, gone, just like Casper. It's funny because Mr. I'm Not Looking For A Relationship thinks you two should become intimate, but yet when you ask him about dating and starting a relationship, he'll say, "I'm not looking for a relationship right now. I'm enjoying my freedom." What the fuck kind of shit is that? Then you ask him why he doesn't even like the word date, he'll say, "I prefer to say we are just hanging out." Okay, motherfucker, you're full of shit, so let me tell you something. I don't fuck people I'm just "hanging out" with, so your sorry ass can just keep it moving. Try that shit on the next woman who doesn't know any better, because I am not the one.

I had a very disappointing experience dealing with Mr. I'm Not Looking For A Relationship. His name was Joseph, and I really liked him. But, later on figured out some things about him I simply could not deal with. First, I noticed him at the credit union where I normally do my banking, not too far from my job.

The first time I noticed him was one day when I was in a rush to deposit a check. He was cute. I wondered what his story was. He seemed like he knew his job pretty well and appeared to have it together. A couple weeks went by, and I saw him again. Then I found myself making excuses to go over to the credit union. One day, I was walking out of my building toward the parking lot when I had the inclination to go to the credit union and see if I could sneak a peek at him. He was packing up his things to leave for the day, so I pretended to be in the lobby filling out some forms. He noticed me just as I wanted him to. As he was walking toward the door, he greeted me. We stood in the lobby and talked for about fifteen minutes or so. He was asking me a little about myself, where I lived, where I worked, etc. I told him I worked right down the street near the Verizon Center. He told me he lived in Bowie, Maryland, had a four-year-old son, and he was raised in Bronx, New York. His accent told me he was a New Yorker! I loved the way they talk. There's something sexy about it. I could tell he wanted my phone number, but I didn't feel right offering it. He went out of his way to tell me he was single, and I told him I was single as well.

I saw him a few more times at the credit union and he would speak to me each time. I think he was a branch manager, because he was always clean cut and in a suit. I stopped and talked to him one day, because I was going to tell him (by throwing hints) I was interested and offer my phone number. I kept getting nervous and couldn't bring myself to do it. I can't stand that about myself. Every time I see a fine man, I get nervous and my speech gets weird and jumbles up. He gave me a tour of the credit union, and telling me about some of his responsibilities. I didn't hear too much of what he was saying because I was too busy fantasizing about him and sizing him up. I saw his lips moving, but heard nothing. His broad shoulders and chocolate skin really had me mesmerized. I completely zoned his voice out and began to fantasize. Snap out of it girl and breathe, I told myself. I was going to pass the hell out if I hadn't taken a breath! I snapped out of my fantasy and came back to reality.

One day, I finally worked up the nerve to give him my phone number. He called while I was in Dallas, Texas attending a conference. When I returned home, I called him and we started seeing each other. We went to see Tyler Perry's *Why Did I Get Married* and it was good. We had a good time. On the drive home, he decided he would ask me some questions. He wanted to know why I was attracted to him.

"So, you like me huh?"

I took a deep breath. I didn't want him to know he had caught me off guard with his sudden question. "I've ran across lots of jerks in my life and you seem to not be one of them, and I think you are a nice guy."

He was very good at figuring people out because he had me down to a science in only a couple weeks.

"Thank you. I think you're a very good person, a little shy, very organized and structured. Now, I must ask you this: What are you looking for?"

"In a word, a relationship."

I guess my answer really shocked him, because he stared at me strangely before he responded.

"Well, I'm not really looking for a relationship, but if you want to hang out with me that's fine."

Here we go again with this shit. What was it with guys and that relationship word?

My heart dropped into my stomach. At that point, my feelings were hurt and I felt stupid for being out with him. I figured it was no use going after someone who didn't want to be caught, so I decided to back off completely. He noticed right away.

He called me one evening and told me I gave up too fast, and he realized he probably scared me off with his relationship comment. He clarified the comment by saying, "Just because I don't want one right now doesn't mean I wouldn't ever want one." I guess this was positive for me, although at first, it sounded like bullshit. He came over a few times and I was so nervous the first time. I had to have a glass of wine to calm myself down. He gave me a nice hug when he left.

As time passed, I found him to be very boring. Lucky for me, it didn't take me long to figure out we weren't going to go very far. He was the kind of person who didn't like going too many places. He was calling me a lot in the beginning, and then I found myself calling him the most. He wouldn't call me back either until the next day, which was a problem for me. It's as if he didn't care. Marilyn said I'm too hard on guys with the telephone thing. My girl Kathy always said I should treat people the way I expect to be treated, and I agree with her totally. I'm not going to chase after any man. There is too much dick out here for me to be chasing after one man. If they don't call me back when I call them, fuck 'em! If they take a long ass time to call me back, then guess what? I'm going to take my sweet time calling them back, too! I'm so sick of this dumb shit with men and the telephone.

Another thing that really irritated me with Joseph was the lack of phone communication. I'm like this: If I call you, call me back. Not three days or a week later either. Show me the common courtesy by, at least, calling me back. Even if you only stay on the phone with me for five minutes, I would appreciate that more than never calling me back. It was just plain ol' fuckin' rude! This dude had a major problem using the telephone. If I called him, he would call back a few days later or sometimes not at all. I found myself calling him more and saying things like, "Did you get my message?" He would say "Yeah, but..." and then proceed to give me some sorry ass excuse I did not want to hear. After a while, I stopped calling him. He would immediately notice and call me saying, "I haven't heard from you in a while."

"Are your damn fingers broke or something? You can call me too sometimes, you know," was always my reply.

I understand the average man does not like talking on the phone, but will it kill them just to pick up the phone every other day for five minutes just to tell their significant other they are thinking about them, or just even to say hello? Notice I said every other day and not every day, because everyone needs a little space. The little things like this will make any relationship sweeter. They know how to call you when they want some ass though, right?

I also figured out Joseph wasn't a very affectionate person. Dude never even touched me.

The one day he showed me an inch of affection was when we were looking at some comedy show on television, and he asked me to sit up beside him. We were snuggled up on the couch and I think he was uncomfortable, getting tempted, or something, because fifteen minutes later, we were damn near sitting at opposite ends of the couch. I was enjoying our cuddling time, but then he got up. Said he had to go home. I didn't want him to leave and I know he could tell. He came over a couple more times and after a while, I was getting a little tired of this, because if we were supposed to be getting to know each other, we should have been doing other things besides just sitting in the house.

I asked him out on another date, because I figured he wasn't going to ask me any time soon, so I made a move. He told me he didn't want to call it a date. He wanted to call it hanging out. That pissed me off to no end. Here's another nigga that doesn't want to use the word "date." He wanted to refer to us as "hanging out." Well fuck, I deserved better than that shit. I called him later on that evening and cancelled the date, without an explanation. Fuck him! He didn't deserve one.

I was blown like a mug! My feelings were not so much hurt, but I was just *so* disappointed, because I really liked him and thought he was different from the other men I'd encountered. I really thought I could have had something with him. I'm glad I found him out early on, instead of getting my feelings involved, and having sex with this dude. I would have felt like a used piece of trash and it would have been much, much harder to let go.

Now, I knew I had to sever my ties with him. I could still be his friend but nothing more. I was wrestling with what I was going to do about him. I won't settle for less than I believe I deserve and if it means me being by myself a while longer than so be it.

I saw this quote somewhere before and it said something like, *If you settle for less, you will end up with less than what you settled for.* That is so true, which was why I'm wasn't going to do it. I was very disappointed in the way that had turned out. I have the worst luck with men. I don't understand why this keeps happening to me. I feel like I am the Joan (from *Girlfriends*) of all my friends. I'm always the one who ends up with no man. I know no one is perfect, but Joseph had too many flaws I didn't want to deal with them and I felt I shouldn't have to deal with him or his flaws.

Mr. I'm Separated From My Wife is another example of the type of man I prefer not to deal with. This dude thinks he's so slick. He lies and tells you he's separated from his wife, and has been separated for a while. This is the biggest scam yet they try to use to get you. If he is separated and does not intend to get back with the wife, then why is he still married to her? Ladies, I don't care how long this dude is singing this song about he's separated don't fall for it.

Change the damn station! Don't walk, but RUN as far away
from him as you can, because you know what's going to happen?
He's going to string you along for a very long time and continue
to tell you he's separated. For all you know, he could be still living
with his wife, fuckin' his wife or not even separated at all. It could
all just be a big fat lie. No matter how you slice it, dice it or chop
it up, getting involved with a married man is wrong. Did you
notice that all he gave you was his cell phone and work number?
Did you also notice he can't spend the night with you, or his
time is very limited? Married men don't have much time for the
chick on the side. You will be alone on holidays, his birthday,
your birthday and other important days. Ladies, it's not worth
it. Don't share dick! You deserve better. Just put yourself in
the wife's place. Would you want someone to be fucking your
husband? Doesn't sound fair, does it? Because it's not. It will last
for a little while, but there is no future with a married man. After
a while, dude is going to reconcile with his wife and your heart is
going to be broken. Then you will be the one feeling like a dumb
ass for seeing a married man.

My little sister got involved with Mr. I'm Separated From My
Wife. She was sprung from day one. She's the baby of the family
and very spoiled. She acts as if the world owes her something.
She can be quite annoying at times. We all have the same curly
hair and medium brown features. She's the only one of us with
gray eyes and we have no idea where the hell they came from.
Our brother, Allen, and I used to tease her all the time growing
up by telling her that her father was a white man. She would

believe us, and she would go crying to Mom. Mom used to fuss at us and tell us to stop that non-sense before she smacked the piss out of us both. It must be down the family tree somewhere.

Ashley's about my size, but a few inches taller than I am. She's only twenty-three, so she had to learn for herself. I kept telling her to leave that nigga alone, but she wouldn't listen to me. They were both wrong. He was a married man and she was the chick on the side. He spent a lot of time and money on my sister in the beginning, but when it came down to the important events in her life like her college graduation, birthday, and the celebration party for her acceptance into one of the biggest and best graduate and law schools in the world he couldn't be there. This girl finished her Bachelor's Degree at Howard at twenty-one, then continued on to Harvard for her Master's Degree, and is currently still there pursuing her law degree. She's going to be a brilliant attorney one day. This is what disappointed me so much about Ashley. For her to be so smart, she sure as hell doesn't have any common sense. She met this loser in one of her law classes. He was older than she was (in his early thirties), so I guess he knew he could run game on her. He also failed to tell her he was married. From the things she was telling me about him, I figured out he was married. When I told her she didn't believe me, and dismissed the thought for months. I remember being on the phone with her one day, because she was frustrated with him for standing her up for one of their dates.

"Shayla, I'm so fuckin mad with him, I don't know what to do!"

"What did Mr. Wonderful do this time, Ash?"

"Girl, he is late again for our date. He said he would be here at five and it's now six."

"And you're still there waiting for him? Girl, I would be gone!"

"He'll be here; he probably got caught in traffic."

"Ash, do you have this guy's home number?"

"Nah, just his cell phone number."

"Have you ever been to his house?"

"Nope, he's always picked me up on campus. What's with all the questions, sis?"

"You may not want to hear this, Ash, but this guy is either married or living with another woman."

"Shay, he is married, but he and his wife are separated."

"I wouldn't have shit to do with that fool until he's divorced! He being separated is dangerous ground for you. He could be lying. If he has nothing to hide, then you should have a home number for him."

"He lives with his cousins, and doesn't want them in his business."

"You believe that bullshit? Please tell me you're not falling for that?"

"He has no reason to lie. He's even introduced me to his boys."

"That doesn't mean shit, girl. Don't you know anything?"

"I guess not as much as you, Miss Know-It-All!" Click.

That little bitch hung up on me. I was blown. She had never done that before. I must have really hit a nerve with her.

After several months of this nonsense, Ashley decided to confront Mr. Wonderful about his living situation and his supposed separation. That slick bastard stuck to his story and insisted he and Ashley not let this little problem interfere with their relationship. Ashley decided this was wrong, even if he was separated. The fact remained; he was still married. She ended the relationship and he tried his best to get her back, but was unsuccessful. My little sister had finally come to her senses. I was so proud of her. Besides, a lot of his story was not adding up. He could never spend the night with her. Now, if he's a grown ass man living with his cousins, why was he rushing off to go home? She still didn't have a home number. Now, if he were living with these cousins, as he told her, and he really was separated from his wife, why would they mind if he gave the number out to someone he's dating? He's never shown up to any of her special events. He always gave her an excuse as to why he couldn't make it. The main excuse he had was that he was studying for his bar exam. The most suspicious thing to me was the fact that they had limited time they spent together. They were only together a minimum of two days a week and sometimes on the weekends.

My take on the whole situation is that dude was lying from the jump. He saw that my sister was young and inexperienced and he knew he could play her. He did for a while, but not as long as he would have liked. With a little coaching from her big sister, she dropped that loser like a bad habit. I knew his face was tight when she told him she was on to him. I would have loved to be a fly on the wall when she told him. She called me to apologize for hanging up on me and informed me of what she planned to do. I gave her blow-by-blow instructions on how to break his ass down!

Mr. I'm Married and Miserable is even slicker than Mr. I'm Separated From My Wife. This nigga expects to see you any time he feels like it and still has to go home to his wife at night. He tells you he's just hanging in there for the kids' sake. That is such bullshit. My parents divorced when I was young and I got over it. Children are tougher than we think they are. They will adjust. As long as the father stays involved in the kids' lives, then there won't be a problem. When a married man approaches me, I rip his ass up with my words. They think I'm crazy after I cussed their asses out. They give me their sad story and I don't believe a word of it. Okay, if you are so miserable then get out. Why the hell are you still in a miserable marriage? Why live your life like that? That is crazy. Married people tell me all the time, "It's not that simple. It's hard to get out of..." FUCK! If I'm miserable, guess what? I'm rolling out! Life is too short to be miserable. People like them make me not ever want to get married. When Mr. I'm Married and Miserable approaches me, I tell them both right off the bat that I don't date married men. It's wrong. Some of these idiots view it as a challenge. I also tell them they should be ashamed of themselves for being on the prowl for women when they have one at home. And then he doesn't get the hint. He keeps asking you out repeatedly as if he's going to get a different answer from the last ten times he's asked you. Give up already! It's not going to happen. Go home to your damn wife!

Bianca's Thoughts:

Men and women are really good at leading double lives, so be careful. Watch the actions of the person you are dating to avoid being played for a fool. It may not be obvious at first, but as time goes on, you will notice a change in their behavior. Not being able to spend the night with them is a big red flag. If a person is only involved with you, then there should be no issues with spending the night. Pay attention to the excuses they give you when the subject of spending the night comes up. Make sure you have their address and HOME phone number, not just a cell phone or work phone number. If that's all you have, then they are more than likely hiding something. If you can't go visit them at their house, something is wrong. Also, if they pick fights with you for bizarre or stupid reasons, then they probably did it so they could spend time with their main love. Pay attention! People are slick!

Is Life Passing You By?

Is life passing you by? Then why do you just sit on that couch
    sometimes and cry
Feeling sorry for yourself because you're alone, and still asking
    yourself why
Is life really passing you by?

I would say so, because you don't really do anything anymore
But sit home and daydream and wonder what life has in store
Is life really passing you by?

Yep, it sure is, because you are still waiting for that dream to
    come true
That dream of you and him being together again and starting
    a new
Is life really passing you by?

It sure is, because even though he loves you, he still won't
    commit
And although you've tried and tried, you can't seem to forget
Is life really passing you by?

Yes, it is, and will you have days where you won't feel so blue?
Are you dreaming a dream that will never come true?
Is life really passing you by?

Chapter Three

MY BEST MALE FRIEND

N ow that I'm done reminiscing, maybe I can focus on my work. I just can't stay focused today for some reason. It's two o'clock and the cable people still haven't shown up. I should cuss their asses out when they get here. Not that I don't like working from home, but this is ridiculous. I've been sitting here all day. The doorbell rings and its Comcast. I open the door with an attitude.

"Mrs. Richardson?"

"No, Johnny Come Lately!" I snapped at him. "It's Ms. Richardson! It's about time you showed up!"

"Sorry, we had a lot of service calls in your area today, Ms. Richardson. This won't take too long."

I closed the door behind him as he was bringing in the rest of his equipment.

"Can you show me which bedroom you need the cable jack in?" he asked politely.

"Sure, follow me."

We go upstairs and I show him the guest room. He starts his work and I go back downstairs to continue with mine. I feel kind of bad now, because he's so nice and polite and I'm acting like a bitch toward him. I'm going to apologize when he comes back downstairs. Maybe I'll even offer him something to eat.

I'm distracted by the television. My soaps are on, so that grabs my attention for a few minutes. I love watching *The Young and the Restless*. I've been watching it since I was a small child. Victor and Jack are so damn funny! I think it's hilarious the way they've been feuding all these years and the way Jack calls Victor "The Mustache," "The Black Knight," and "The Great Man." I told my godmother it's her fault I'm addicted to soaps. She watched me when I was little while my mom was at work. I remember we used to sit up on her bed and watch the soaps. I would be in my pajamas and she would be trying to get me to take a nap. She'd be tickling me and doing everything she could do to tire me. It didn't work though. Being the inquisitive little child I was, I wanted to watch, too. Other days, we would be downstairs in her living room watching the soaps. One day, when we were watching a soap on TV, Amy was with Tyrone and he was living a double life, trying to put on makeup to pass himself off as a white man. How the hell he did that, I have no idea. I don't even remember. When I talk to my mom about that today, she's surprised that I remember. Nikki has not aged a bit since she's been on the show. I still can't believe The Mustache picked her up in a strip club. I guess Victor had to get his freak on, too. He rescued her from that life and made her into the woman she is today. Another person that hasn't aged much is Brad. He is still fine as hell! He's a nasty bastard though. How are you going to be married to two sisters? He married Traci, had a child with her, then some years later, he married her sister Ashley. I love Michael Baldwin's character, too. He has the smart ass, snappy comeback lines that I love. He reminds me a lot of myself actually. I also like Jill. She is a trip. I'll never forget the episode when Leanna cut her hair and she told her she was practically bald. Her hair was only cut shoulder length. That was funny as hell.

I hear footsteps coming down the stairs, so I turn the television down a little.

"All done, Ms. Richardson," the tall, light-skinned man said in a deep voice. He was doing his paperwork and seemed to be in a hurry to leave. I don't blame the man. Especially after the way I had acted. He had good posture, nice arms and a nice chest. He either has been to jail, in the military or just works out often.

"If you would please sign here, I'll be on my way," he said, handing me the clipboard and a pen.

I signed my name beside the big red X as slow as I could, because I wanted to keep him here a little longer, just so I could look at him. I handed the clipboard back to him and began to apologize.

"Listen, I'm very sorry for the way I acted earlier. I know it's not your fault. Comcast is a very large company and I know you have tons of customers, not just me."

"No problem, Ms. Richardson. I'm used to it. I get yelled at all the time. Apology accepted." He gave me a nice smile. I heard an accent similar to mine.

"Hey, where are you from?"

"I'm from Alabama. Why do you ask?"

"Oh, because I heard an accent. Country people can always tell when we run across one of our own!"

"You got that right, Miss. Where are you from?"

"Born and raised in Charlotte, North Carolina."

"I knew I heard an accent on you, country girl," he says, giving me a playful punch on my arm.

We both start laughing and our eyes locked.

"Hey, do you want something to eat? You know us country folks are always feeding people, right?"

"Yes indeed, I know. Sure, I'll have something to eat. That is so nice of you, Ms. Richardson."

"Please, call me Shay. Hey, I just realized that I didn't get your name."

"Daniel," he says with a grin.

"It's biblical, of course. All of my brothers and sisters have biblical names."

"That's cool, Daniel."

He warmed up to me quickly. A few minutes ago, he was trying to get the hell out of dodge. I'm glad I apologized. I can tell he really appreciated it."

"Whatchu got to eat on, Shay?"

"Oh, just some leftovers from last night. Just some baked chicken with gravy, sweet potatoes, greens and cornbread."

"Damn, girl! Who were you cooking for, the cast of *Soul Food?*"

I start laughing and give him a playful punch like the one he gave me earlier. I couldn't believe I was about to feed a total stranger. But as I said, that's just how we country folks are.

I fixed us both a plate and he went to the bathroom to wash his hands. I didn't realize I hadn't eaten yet. It was true what they said about skinny people forgetting to eat. He returned and we both parked ourselves in front of the television and watched the rest of *The Young and the Restless*. We bowed our heads and said grace. When I lifted my head, he was all into the show. He looked interested in the soap and seemed to know what was going on.

"Oh my gosh! You watch this?" I said surprised.

"Yeah, girl, this is my show! My grandmother and I used to watch this all the time when I was little," he said, taking a fork full of his food.

"No kidding! I'm surprised dudes watch soaps."

"Yes indeed, dudes watch soaps. They might try to front like they don't, but some of us do. My brothers tease me because I watch it."

I giggle a little at his comments. Oh my goodness, he's really into this. I can't believe I'm sitting here with this nice looking brother watching soaps and he's interested in it as much as I am. Wow, this is wild.

"Is Mrs. Chancellor still on here?"

"Yep, you know she's not going anywhere. She's been on here for years."

"Jill is always getting smart with somebody," he says somewhat annoyed with her character.

"I love Jill. She's got the best comeback lines on here."

"She's a whore! She's been with a lot of men on this show."

I start to laugh my ass off at Daniel. He is too funny.

"Daniel, she hasn't been with that many men, has she?"

"Come on, Shay, are you kidding? Do you really need me to break it down for you?"

I rolled my eyes and turned my lips up at him as he continued to argue his point.

"She was with Philip Chancellor, who was Mrs. Chancellor's husband 'til she stole him from her. She's been married to John Abbott, a couple times I think. She's been with Jack, Mr. Abbott's son, which is triflin' and nasty as hell. Then she's also been with Brad, Victor and Larry Wharton! Larry rocked her world though."

"Okay, I take that back, she has been with a lot of men, you're right. I almost forgot all about her being with Jack. Only on the soaps, huh?"

"Not always. Sometimes that stuff happens in real life, too," he says, still enjoying his food.

Little did I know I would later on find out why he made that comment.

"How's the food, Daniel?"

"Girl, this food is off the chain! Leftovers my ass! What did you put in these sweet potatoes?"

"If I tell you, I'll have to kill you! It's a secret."

"Come on, please! Let me know what are in these that make them so good."

"Okay, I'll tell you on one condition."

"What's that?"

"When you make them, you have to bring me some!"

"Oh, sure, that's not a problem. I'll be happy to bring you some. Now what's in it?" he said excitedly.

"First of all, can you cook? I can't be giving up the secret to the recipe if you're going to burn it."

"Girl, please. I'm from the dirty south! Of course I can cook. I've been cooking since you've been in your daddy's nut sack," he said with his face frowned up.

I bust out laughing at him. Daniel is comical. He became comfortable around me quick.

"Alright dude, the secret is brown sugar, cinnamon, and syrup. Not that plain ol' maple syrup either, it has to be King Syrup."

"King syrup? You mean that thick ass syrup that takes forever to come out of the bottle?"

"Yep, that would be the one! Trust me; this is the main ingredient. If you don't use King Syrup, it won't turn out right."

"For real?"

"Yep! If you use that runny stuff, it's going to be nasty. It won't taste like mine."

"Do you use that syrup for anything else?"

"Umm, yeah! Have you heard of pancakes and French toast?"

"Yes I have. You use that syrup on your pancakes? That stuff is too thick for me."

"We've been eating King Syrup for years. The only time I use the thin runny stuff is when the grocery store is out of King Syrup."

We finished watching *The Young and the Restless* and I take our plates and put them in the sink. I'm having a good time with Daniel. I need to figure out a way to get his number. I'm panicking as I rinse our plates, trying to come up with a plan. This man is on the clock, he has to get back to work soon. Come on, Shayla Janae Richardson, think! Hmm... I could tell him I have another cable jack for him to install. That way, he'll have to come back! Nah, girl, that is stupid and so high school! Think, girl!

I return to the living room and Daniel has dozed off right there on my couch. Just like black folks. Get their belly full then fall asleep! I laugh to myself. He's stretched out on my couch as if he hasn't had a good night's sleep in weeks. I cover him with a blanket and move to the other couch to get back to work. He slept for two hours. I started to wake him, but he looked so peaceful.

I hear him moan a little as I look up from my laptop. He looks around the room at first, as if he doesn't know where he is.

"Yo, how long have I been sleep?" he says, sitting up slowly.

"A couple hours," I say with a smile.

"I'm so sorry I fell asleep on your couch for that long, my bad."

"No need to apologize, Daniel. You were obviously tired. I contemplated waking you, but you were sleeping so peacefully. I hope you don't get into any trouble."

"Nah, it's all good. You were my last service call of the day, thank God."

"I'm glad then. I would hate for you to get in trouble because I didn't wake you."

"Shayla, I feel like I've known you for a long time and I've only known you for about four hours, right?"

"Yep, it's wild, ain't it? How we country folks just embrace each other with open arms."

Daniel is mad cool! I don't know the last time I've had this much fun in my house with a stranger. I definitely want to keep in touch with him. He's so warm and friendly. I would have never thought he was this cool.

"Well, I'm going to take off and let you finish your work. Thanks for everything, especially them sweet potatoes!"

We both bust out laughing, then our eyes lock again. He leans down and gives me a kiss on the cheek, then gives me the biggest, tightest hug I've ever had. He writes his numbers on a piece of paper and hands it to me.

"Please call me sometime, country girl! I would like to stay in touch with you."

"Okay, sure," I say, blushing.

He left and I finished my work for the day and logged off my laptop.

ൟ   ൟ   ൟ

I drive into work the next morning feeling good. Waking up in a good mood, so that means I drive to work. I park two blocks from my building and give the parking attendant my key.

Inside the office, Marilyn is already hard at work.

"Good morning, lady."

"Hey, girl, how was your day yesterday, working from home?"

"It was very interesting and peaceful. I got a lot accomplished, plus the cable jack is finally in the guest room. Now Ashley can stop complaining about no cable being in the guest room when she brings her spoiled ass here for visits. Is there any coffee made?"

"Of course! You know we are all coffee addicts around here," she says with a laugh.

I get situated at my desk before heading for the coffee area. Before I turn the corner, I hear voices. It sounds like that annoying ass Deborah. Deborah is a different kind of person. Everyone knows she is a little nuts, but she is our chief financial officer and has the biggest staff in the company. A lot of people are intimidated by her, but I sure as hell am not and she knows it. I put that bitch in her place a long time ago. Every since I did, I haven't had a problem out of her. She is in her mid-forties and married with three kids. She is one of those women who have to have her career straight first, and then have kids. She waited way too late to have kids, if you ask me. Her kids are very young. I believe the oldest one is only four years old. That's insane! I'll be damned if I'm going to be trying to be somebody's mother at fuckin' forty years old. If I don't have any children by the time I reach thirty-five, then I guess I won't be having any. I move a little closer, but stay around the corner so she wouldn't see me. I peek and see Deborah, and she is having a conversation with Jennifer, one of our interns. It is more like an interrogation. She is asking that girl all kinds of personal questions and talking down to her. Jennifer works in the advertising department and she is one of the best interns we have. She's around twenty years old, a junior at University of the District of Columbia and has a two-year-old daughter. For Deborah, this is just terrible in her eyes, and feels Jennifer is too young to have a two-year-old.

"Jennifer, did you want to have a baby?" she asks sarcastically.

Jennifer gives her a strange look. "It wasn't planned if that's what you're asking." Jennifer sounds really annoyed, as she makes another pot of coffee for us addicts.

"You know, when I was eighteen, I was too busy thinking about my career, not having a baby. My goodness, you were only a child yourself, what did your parents have to say?"

"My parents didn't say anything because I was a grown woman and taking care of myself!" she retorts.

"But, honey, you are only twenty years old. What about college? Are you going to finish? Is somebody helping you take care of your daughter?"

I have heard enough. I am going to confront Deborah.

"Okay, Deborah, that's enough! Don't you *ever* talk to her that way again! This girl is one of the best interns we have. She comes to work on time, she's working hard in school, hell, she's on the dean's list, and she's taking care of a child. It's none of your fuckin' business why she had a child at eighteen. It's not her fault you waited until you were damn near a senior citizen to start having kids. Everybody's life is not based on yours, Deborah. We are all different. Come to think of it, I think you are a little envious of her because she had her child decades before you had yours!"

Deborah is in such a shock, she can hardly speak. Jennifer is in the background, looking on and surprised as well.

"After all that shit you just talked to Jennifer, don't you have anything to say now?"

Deborah gives me a phony smile and replies, "I have work to do. Chat with you ladies later." She storms off in a big hurry.

Jennifer starts to walk toward me. "Thank you so much, Ms. Richardson, for standing up for me. That lady is really a piece of work, isn't she?"

I smile and put my hand on her shoulder.

"Sweetie, you can call me Shayla, and yes, that bitch is a piece of work. As long as I'm around here, I guarantee you that you won't have a problem out of her again."

She smiles and looks at ease. "Thanks again, Shayla," she says, walking down the hall.

I get my coffee fix and head back to my office. On the way there, I'm thinking about Jennifer; she is so strong. I don't think I could raise a child and go to college. Shoot, college is stressful enough. When I think about the will of this young woman to finish school and succeed, my heart goes out to her, because it has to be hard dealing with all of that plus a child. I think Jennifer is going to be my employee when she finishes college. That's exactly the kind of person I need on my team. I surely will not forget her.

Bianca's Thoughts:

Male friends are some of the best friends a woman can have. When you need male advice and go to your girlfriends, most of the time, they are going to tell you "Oh, forget all about him, he ain't shit" or "you should do this," or "you should do that." It's totally different when you talk to a guy for advice. They give you a totally different side and they put a different spin on it. A lot of my best advice has come from my male friends. I love it! I love my girlfriends, but it's easier to talk to my male friends. They probably tell me some stuff they shouldn't because it breaks "the man code," but it has really helped me through some tough situations and for that, I will be forever grateful to them.

Chapter Four

I NEED A TUNE-UP

It's been months since I've had sex and I'm about to go crazy. Normally, I could hold out for long periods of time, but it's starting to get to me for some reason. I have a couple of maintenance men I could call, but I always feel like a dirty little whore when I'm done with them. I'm trying to think whom I can call. Whom would I want to call? Who's the best? I pull out my little book to see which guys have the highest rating. Everyone I've ever had sex with got a rating from 1 to 10, with 10 being the highest, of course. The closer the person is to 10, the better. I only have two 10s on this list and one of them is about to get a phone call. It's not as if I've had many sex partners either. Now, that's a low number.

I flip through my book and run across Michael's number. He got a 10. Michael is dark-skinned with a low haircut, standing about six feet three inches, has a deep seductive voice and is just fine as hell. The only negative thing about him is he was badly hurt by an ex-girlfriend and vowed never to get involved in a relationship again. I knew that when I first met him, so I don't expect too much. As time went on though, I did develop some feelings for him.

When we first met, I went to his house a couple of times during the NBA playoffs because we are both basketball fans. We had so much fun together. It was almost like hanging out with one of my homeboys, but a little different. Even though I cared for him, I had to dismiss any thoughts I had in my head about becoming his girlfriend, because I'm not in the business of trying to change people. So, I knew straight up we would never have anything more than a sexual relationship. I wasn't that cool with that either.

I start dialing Michael's number. It rings about four times and I was about to hang up.

"Hello," he answers in that deep sexy voice.

"Hey, Michael, what's up? It's Shayla."

"What's up, stranger? How you been?" He sounds like he is surprised to hear from me. I guess he could be, since it's been about four months since we last spoke.

"I'm doing great, and you?"

"Hey, I can't complain, love. So what you getting into tonight?"

"Nothing much, just chillin'."

"You want some company?"

Damn, he's making this too easy. I don't even have to ask.

"Sure, that sounds good." I say, trying not to sound pressed.

"A'ight, I will be there around eight, if that is okay."

"Eight is perfect. I'll see you then."

I look at the clock; it is after six, so I have more than enough time to do my usual ritual before my rendezvous. I relax in the tub for almost an hour, while enjoying a glass of White Zinfandel and listening to slow jams on my little stereo in the bathroom. That always seems to relax me and get me in the mood before one of my rendezvous. After my bath, I moisturize in cucumber melon lotion, slip on my favorite silk robe, put on some soft music and pour myself another glass of wine. As soon as I take one sip, the doorbell rings. That has to be Michael. I open the door, and there he is. That tall, sexy, chocolate man is standing in my doorway, looking at me seductively like he is about to eat me for dinner. He reminds me a bit of Morris Chestnut.

"What's up, love? Nice to see you," he says, hugging me tight.

Michael always calls me love and makes me feel special. Even though I know damn well he doesn't love me. That was just his pet name for me, I guess.

"It's really good to see you, too. Man, it's been a while. Come on in."

"Yes it has; you want to tell me what's up with that," he says, sitting on the couch.

He sounds somewhat serious, as if he really wants an explanation as to why he hasn't heard from me.

"Well, you know, I've been really busy with work and stuff. There's a lot going on there."

"Really?" he says slowly, raising his eyebrows.

Now this is different. I wonder why he is sitting here interrogating me. What the hell? He ain't my man, and I ain't his woman, so he better chill.

"Yeah, really." I shot back at him. "My job can be quite stressful at times."

"A'ight, girl, if you say so." He sounded annoyed.

Okay, he is really fuckin' up the mood right now. I had better change the subject quick before I get pissed!

So, finally, he starts kissing me on the neck and getting the foreplay started. I couldn't believe he went from angry to romantic in like five seconds. He started rubbing my pussy, so I knew what that meant. He was ready! Yes! He put his head under my robe and went to work licking my pussy. Oh my God, it felt *soooo* good. I started to moan uncontrollably. He loved that shit. He really knows his way around a pussy. Damn. He had me so wet already; I couldn't believe it. He slides a condom on and put himself inside me.

"Uhhh," I moan.

"You okay?" he says with concern.

"Yeah, I'm fine; it's just been a while."

He takes nice slow strokes at first, and then he picks up his pace when he sees how much I am enjoying it. We have been at it for at least an hour. He starts to shake and moan. He must be coming hard.

We lie here for a moment discussing what we want out of life, etc. I tell him I am tired of this every now and then sex thing. It doesn't seem to bother him, but it bothers me. I'm not saying I want to be in a relationship with him, but I do want a relationship with somebody, eventually. But, it looks like he is turning out to be just what he is, a bed buddy. When it dawns on me that this casual sex thing isn't really bothering Michael, I decide it is time for me to sever all ties with him. We have been doing this for a while now, but I am growing tired of it.

Michael gets up, puts his pants on. "Hey, I got an early day tomorrow," he informs me, "so I better get going." His voice was low and full of bullshit.

"Okay, that's cool," I say, my response nonchalant. I don't want his ass to think I am pressed for him to stay the night. As far as I am concerned, he can get the fuck out. I really don't care. As a matter of fact, I am a little messed up in the head.

"Are you okay? You look kind of sad." I can't believe he just said that shit.

"Yeah, I'm fine. Don't you worry about me."

He looks at me strange, and I am trying my best to keep my composure. He finishes dressing and leaves.

Here I am, again. Alone for the night with no one to hold…

ᔖ ᔖ ᔖ

With morning comes another exciting day at work. So far, it has been quiet. The big bosses are at a conference this week, so Marilyn and I pretty much have the entire floor to ourselves.

For some reason, Michael is weighing heavily on my mind. I really think about him a lot. I know he is not relationship material, but hey, a girl can daydream, can't she? I had a wonderful fantasy that he would be ready for the relationship I was so hoping for and we would get married and have a couple of kids. Whom the hell am I kidding? This man is never going to commit. He is too busy having fun. He doesn't want to be tied down with a girlfriend.

"Shayla!" Marilyn calls out to me. I must have been staring into space. "Dang, girl, what is on your mind today?"

"Girl, its Michael. He came over last night and you know what happened so don't even ask," I whisper.

"Did you have an argument with him or something, because you look really down?"

"Nah, it was nothing like that. I mean, Michael is a nice person and all, but he doesn't want a relationship and I have to accept that. Besides, I'm getting really tired of this little sexual thing we have going. You know I'm not the casual sex type."

"Yeah, I know you aren't, but don't put too much energy into this guy, especially since you already know what he's about. I'm not saying he's not nice, Shayla, but if he's not looking for the same thing you are, I think you are better off without him."

"I was thinking the same thing on the way in this morning. I'm getting to that age where I want to be married and having kids. I'm not trying to be like Miss Thing on the fourth floor and wait 'til I'm in my damn forties to start having kids. I really don't want to do that. I do think it's best I sever my ties with him. I'm going to call him tonight and tell him."

"You're making the right decision, girl" Marilyn's voice is gentle.

Marilyn is awesome. She is like the Aunt I wish I had. Always the voice of reason and always there to give me sound advice.

After work, I go home and really think about my sudden interest in being in a relationship with Michael. I know he is no good for me, but I am still fantasizing about the idea anyway. Why do we—women—always want what's not good for us? Michael doesn't really have it all together to be his age. He is about my age, maybe a couple years older, and he still lives with his brother. Mind you, his brother is married and has a family of his own, so imagine that imposition. Now, I think a thirty-something-year-old man has no business living with other people. He should have his own place by now. I had asked him a while back if he's ever had his own place before and he said he did when he was in his twenties. What the fuck? I've had my own place since I graduated from college because it's nice to have your own stuff. Anyway, I guess I needed confirmation from what he and I discussed in the bed the other night, so I call him to see if his "opinion" had changed on relationships. It hadn't, so it is time for me to let him go for good. No more late night rendezvous. I'll write him a nice long "Dear John" letter, explaining why I can no longer see him. I'm sure he will not write me back, and I don't expect him to because he's just that way—nonchalant attitude, especially for things like this.

I did the right thing, yet I feel terrible. I feel lonely and my feelings are hurt because he thought enough of me to have sex with me but not enough to be in a relationship with me. My brother would be so disappointed in me if he knew I was sitting here pining away for this man. I started feeling unworthy of any man's love after the incident with Michael. My self-esteem went down big time. I went into a bit of a depression for a while, because I just couldn't believe he didn't want me. I had to move on though, because you can't make a man want you, and I damn sure am not going to try to convince him or beg his ass. No way, fuck that! He's not the only man on this earth. The only man I'm ever going to beg is Jesus to let me into the pearly gates. Who does he think he is anyway? Morris Chestnut or somebody? Humph....

Bianca's Thoughts:

How are people so caught up in sex to where feelings get involved? Easy! Sex is very emotional for most women and once sex gets involved, so do feelings. It's hard to have sex with someone over a long period and not develop any feelings. Most of us can't have sex with someone over a long period and not develop feelings for that person. Sex is a very emotional thing for most of us women.

Overcoming Fear

Not wanting to become involved too fast
Not wanting to repeat the mistakes from the past

The wall will eventually come down
The nonchalant attitude will come around

Not expecting to care this much
Never forgetting that first or second touch

Butterflies often overwhelming me
Often realizing things I thought I'd never see

Still promising myself not to become involved too fast
While staying confident that I will not repeat mistakes from
    the past

Chapter Five

I'M SO TIRED OF THIS SHIT

I sit on my couch, reminiscing about the recent chain of events that has happened in my life, and I had an "aha" moment: The things you don't sweat are the things you usually end up getting. Like my job. I had two offers on the table at the same time when this job came through. When I interviewed with the managers, I really didn't think I was going to get the job because I was fresh out of college. I mean, I had just graduated the week before. After the interview, I had a couple more to go on and I went to those interviews without giving this one another thought. Well, actually I did wonder a little if I did well and if they liked me, but that's about it. I didn't hear from them for quite some time, so I continued to go on all the interviews I could. I arrived home one day and had two FedEx envelopes on my doorstep. One of them was an offer letter for the job I have now. I didn't sweat it and I got it. The same rule applies to relationships. If I weren't sweating this thing with Michael so hard, I would probably have him. But of course, since I'm worrying about it, I don't have him.

So, here I am. All alone again, reevaluating my life. At my age, I should be married by now with a couple kids running around. I'm starting to wonder if it is ever going to happen for me. When my good friend, Daniel, was going through a situation with his wife, I felt bad for him. She stepped out on him and had an affair. All of his boys kept telling him, "Man, fuck that bitch, blah, blah, blah." He would always talk to me because he knew I would be the gentle and objective one, unlike his boys. I told him his boys were damn idiots and should have never given him advice in the first place. The man was hurt and upset because the woman he had been married to for the last fifteen years had an affair. Can you imagine the pain of that? Well, I'm here to tell you, it doesn't feel good. I've never been married, but I have been cheated on and the pain is indescribable, one you carry with you for a while. It takes time to get over something so painful. It doesn't just go away overnight. Daniel and I had many conversations about his situation and I could really tell that this woman really did a number on him. I told him I would never tell him things like his boys did, because you shouldn't tell someone how they are supposed to feel because you are not them and you really don't know how the person feels. It's easy for someone else to say, "Aw man, you don't need her, just move on with your life," or "Man, you are better off without that trick," etc. Only the person who is going through the drama can make such a call and they have to do it on their own. People are so quick to judge and tell you what "they" would do, when truly what they REALLY need to do is shut the fuck up and let you make your own decision.

I do my part as his friend and am here to listen to him and give him the best advice I possibly can, anytime he needs it. That's what a friend is supposed to do, not tell you "Well, if it were me, I would…." He has come a long way from that incident and he actually had a clean divorce. However, because she hurt him so badly, I have not seen my friend date anyone or even give a woman the time of day. He said he is not ready to date, which is understandable. It has not been that long since all of this happened. Now a man like Daniel would be a good catch for any woman, and he's fine too! He takes care of his twin girls, and spends a lot of time with them. Those twins are *so* cute! Well-mannered and well behaved. Daniel is every woman's dream, and is just an all-around good ol' southern man. This is the kind of husband my girl Monique has, but she surely does not appreciate him. She's a totally different story.

He was looking for her one night last week when she was out on one of her little rendezvous. I told her do not use me as the excuse as to where she was and then not tell me. Her husband called my house, asking me if I knew where she was, and I was caught off guard, but I covered for her. I had drifted off on the couch earlier while watching TV and the sound of the phone woke me.

"Hello," I said, sounding groggy.

"Shayla, did I wake you?"

"Oh, hey Calvin, I had drifted off, but it's cool. How are you?"

66

"I'm good. I'm lookin' for your girl, have you seen her this evening?"

Oh, shit. This damn girl done used me for the alibi and forgot to tell me. Wait until I see her ass.

"Yeah, I saw her earlier, why?"

He took a deep breath before he answered me and he was starting to sound annoyed because he's been down this "disappearing acts" road with Monique's ass before.

"Well, she told me she'd be with you all day, and it's nine o'clock, and she still hasn't made it home yet. I'm starting to get a little worried."

"Oh, you know what Calvin, she did tell me she had a couple of relatives to go visit and that she would come back to my house in a little bit, so I'll have her call you when she gets here."

Okay, that'll work. Thanks, Shayla."

"Not a problem."

I couldn't believe she'd done that. I was going to tell Monique's ass off when I talked to her. I took a deep breath and began to dial her cell phone. It rang about five times but she finally answered.

"Hello," she said, sounding annoyed.

"Girl, your husband just called here looking for you! Look, I don't know what you're doing and really don't give a fuck, but you better get your little ass over here right now and call him. Why didn't you tell me that you told him you'd be with me? He caught me off guard and I gave him an excuse, I just hope he believed it."

My mouth was going a mile a minute and I hardly gave her a chance to get a word in.

"Shayla, calm your ass down, I'll be there shortly" she said, sounding mad.

I don't know why the hell she was sounding all irritated and shit. I should've been the one pissed off. Actually, I was very pissed off at her because I was tired of her shit. She always pulled stunts like that. I wish she would have called me, and then I would have been better prepared to deal with his questions. She doesn't realize how blessed she is. She has a good man, yet she always feels the need to step out on him. I really don't think she realizes how lucky she is, because it sucks to be single. Most of the time, us single people wish we were married, and the married people wish they were single.

A couple of hours later, my doorbell rang and she came storming through the door, looking irritated and acting strange.

"What's wrong, Monique?"

"Girl, my time got cut short and now I gotta go home. Shoot!"

"Girl, what the fuck is wrong with you?" I snapped at her. "You act like you in fuckin' high school or something about to break curfew. You ARE married, but I think sometimes you forget."

"Whatever, Shayla! Let me call Calvin before he goes nuts." She looked back at me and shook her head as she reached over to get the phone.

Thank God, she called her husband and calmed him down. They sounded like they had a few words, but Monique sweet-talked herself out of trouble. She tried to make it seem like she was visiting some cousin of hers in LaPlata. That man is not stupid. He's going to catch her one of these days. She left shortly after she made the call and to be honest with you, I was glad her needy ass was gone! She worked my nerves sometimes. She is my most exhausting friend. She's a handful, that's for sure.

ও ও ও

This whole Michael thing has me tripping. I pour a glass of Arbor Mist White Zinfandel, my favorite wine. I need something to calm my nerves. I am beginning to feel sorry for myself again and getting depressed. This depression thing is getting a little out of hand. I have never gotten this depressed before over a guy. Damn, it's over. I cut it off, so why am I still trippin'? I guess it's because he wasn't ready for what I was offering. He also seemed like the kind of man that wasn't done running yet. You know the type that likes to be out in the street all the time and dating more than one woman at a time. I guess I'm feeling this way because I feel like he used me. We only hooked up for sex. We never really hung out or anything or did things that couples do. Oh my God, listen to me. I think I just realized that I have feelings for him—real deep feelings, too. Aw man, I promised myself I wasn't going to get caught up by him. Shit! I keep trying to tell myself I'm better off without someone like him in my life. You know it's sad, but I actually lie to all my friends and tell them Michael and I are a couple. Either everyone, except Daniel, is married or in relationships and I feel left out. Those who are married tell me I'm better off single and that marriage is a big joke, and I should leave my life the way it is. I'm not sure if I agree with this analogy. It's easy for someone who is married to make a statement like that but for those of us who are still single and unattached it is quite funny.

Another friend of mine told me not to complicate my life with marriage. Instead, she advises me to get what she calls a life partner. In other words, have a long-term relationship without any legal commitments. I really don't see the sense in that either. It's not the route I want to take, but it was interesting to get her opinion as well. I really want to see for myself what marriage is like because I hear so many bad things about it that I really wonder if it is really as bad as people say it is. My brother Allen sure doesn't seem to complain about his marriage at all. In fact, he told me that he is living in marital bliss. Those were his exact words. I know my Mr. Right will come along one day; I just have to be patient.

Bianca's Thoughts:

At some point in your life, you will want to settle down and have someone to come home to every day. Just inviting someone over every now and then will get old fast. You deserve better, you just have to believe it. There's nothing worse than finding someone you are interested in and the other person doesn't share your same goals. If you are into someone more than they are into you, it's never going to work because the other person isn't quite ready for what you are ready for. You are better off letting that person go on about their business because they would be truly just holding you back from the person you are really supposed to be with.

Chapter Six

NOW WHAT?

Now that the whole Michael fiasco is over, now what the hell am I going to do? Am I going to hate all men because of a few that didn't work out the way I wanted it to, become a bitter bitch for the rest of my life, or dust myself off and try again? I try not to fall for people too quick, and sometimes not at all for fear that I may get hurt. Turns out, I did fall for Michael and I'm mad at myself because of it. Damn, my life really sucks right now and I'm tired of this whole being single shit. I'm also tired of people telling me "Oh, Shayla, you're so pretty and you have so much to offer someone, so don't forget it either." Yeah, whatever. Right now, my life as it is tells a different story. A story about a young woman who just can't get this shit right.

I had dinner with Marilyn the other night. She has been concerned about my depression and me and wanted to get me out of the house for a while. For a while now, I've had a problem with depression and sometimes I slip into these depression phases and often times, it takes me a while to come out of it.

This one had been lasting for quite a while, maybe six months. I think this is the longest and roughest one I've had so far. I get in the mood where I'm not talking to anyone and I just want to be left alone. You know it's true what they say about what you see on the outside is not what you really see. You never know what a person is going through by just looking at them. A person can be smiling on the outside and hurting on the inside. That's why it's important to be kind to people because you never know, you may be the one to give them hope to get through their day.

We plan to meet at MaMa Stella's, an Italian restaurant in Clinton and it is nice. I try to convince myself that getting out would be good for me. I meet her at the restaurant and the look on her face says it all. She is worried about me. I just feel like the world's biggest loser right now when it comes to love. Nothing is working out for me in that department and it is really starting to bother me and get to me. I pretend to be sick when I am invited to family functions because I am tired of showing up without a date, when everyone else is with someone; sick of feeling like a "third wheel." It also doesn't help when people ask, "You're not married yet?" or "You don't have a boyfriend?" I really get tired of explaining that one. Oh, my favorite one is when my uncle implied I was gay because "We've never seen you bring a man around us," as he puts it. Oh, so I guess that makes me gay because I won't bring my dates around them. See, that's where he has it twisted. Why bring someone around your family if you don't even know where the relationship is going? He's so ignorant. He's lucky he caught me on a good day, because uncle or not, he was about to get cussed out!

The hostess seated us and the waitress came over shortly thereafter to get our drink orders. We both order wine. I need something to help me relax and prepare for the wisdom Marilyn was about to kick to me.

Marilyn is not only a coworker, but also an awesome friend. She is a wealth of knowledge. She's married with four children. The oldest one is in college.

We get into a deep discussion about my depression; what I should do to get better. She suggested I come with her to church one Sunday, and stay in constant prayer about the situation. Both of us are Christian women, so I understand fully what she was trying to do.

The waitress came back over to take our orders. She orders the lasagna and I order the shrimp pasta.

She leans back in her chair and looks at me with concern. I know something was heavy on her mind.

"Now, Shayla, I have something important to ask you about Michael."

"What's that?" I take a sip of my wine.

"Did you think he was the one for you?"

"No, not really, but it would have been nice to just date him for a while. I did get a little caught up though and developed some feelings for him."

"I want you to really analyze this situation good though," she says, nodding her head.

"What do you mean?"

"Well, Michael is one of those men with a wounded heart, so it's going to take him a long time to want to be with someone else, so don't be too hard on yourself. It wasn't your fault it didn't work out. Michael is still out here playing around and trying to screw everything that moves. You really don't need someone like that in your life and someone like that eventually cheats on you. You're too nice of a person to settle for a dude like him. He wasn't the one for you."

"Yeah, Marilyn, I hear what you're saying, but it's really hard being by myself."

"I understand, Shayla, but Michael wasn't available to you all the time. You only got bits and pieces of his time. Now, let's say you married him. Do you think that would change?"

I shook my head no.

"Okay, so not only would it not change, but now it's going to hurt more because he's your husband and you are going to expect him to spend time with you the way a husband should." She pauses and looks at me before she continues. It's like she wants to make sure I really understand what she is saying.

"Girl, I know it is rough out here trying to date and stuff, because I have nieces your age dealing with the same things and I want you all just to be patient and be strong. God is going to send you the man you are supposed to have, the man He wants you to have and when that man comes, I want you to be ready. I want you to keep an open mind and not focus so much on their looks, but look at their heart."

The waitress comes with our food and we eat a little as we continue to talk. Marilyn says her lasagna is really good and my shrimp pasta is the bomb! When the waitress returns to check on us, I order another glass of wine. I need it, because Marilyn is getting rather deep on me.

"I want to tell you something about marriage, Shayla."

"Okay," I say, relaxing in my chair a bit.

"Marriage is a lot of work. It is not easy. You have to pick your battles and not argue over little petty stuff. Make sure you get someone who really loves God, because if he loves God then he will know how to love you. That person should want the best for you and not try to compete with you. I want you to be really careful when you pick a husband because I know you and if you get with the wrong person that gets on your nerves all the time, you will be like 'Uhhh uh, Ms. Marilyn, I am not doing this!'" she says, bursting into laughter.

I laugh aloud at that, too, because it was the truth. She does know me well and I will drop somebody in a minute.

"Just make sure you pick the right person, honey, because it's an easy thing to get into, but it's hard to get out of. I want you to try marriage for yourself so you can see what it's all about. I'm not telling you not to ever get married; you have to make that decision for yourself."

"I feel you, Marilyn. I will surely keep everything in mind that you have said tonight. Thanks so much for caring and for being a true friend."

"You're more than welcome," she said as she took a sip of her wine.

We linger at the restaurant for a while longer and continue to talk before we call it a night.

I was just about ready to start looking into taking a leave of absence because of my depression. I started calculating how much my bills were per month and whether or not I could afford to live off 60% of my salary because that is what long-term disability would pay me. I checked my employee handbook and there were too many things I would have to explain to human resources, which I felt was none of their business. This information was necessary though in order for me to take a leave of absence. I figured I would only need a month or two to get myself together. My work wasn't as stellar as it used to be and at times, I found it difficult to concentrate and get things done. I had to do something because this was really getting out of hand. It was strange how I would be watching TV and one of those depression medication commercials would come on. Humph, maybe medication can help me. After reading everything in the employee handbook about what I needed to do, I decided against taking a leave of absence. On a professional level, it was too risky. I didn't want to be viewed as crazy or as someone who lost control of her life. Instead, I decided to take a few days off, attend church more regularly than I have been and, of course, stay in constant prayer as Marilyn recommended.

So far so good. It's been a few months, and God really works fast! My depression is much better, I did not need medication or a leave of absence and my outlook on things is a lot better now.

Another weekend is here and I have a few things going on. To better myself, I have also been making an effort to get out more. Since I had been cooped up in the house for quite a while, I decided to break that habit. My weekends aren't normally this busy; in fact, I don't really do too much. Sometimes, I will give my brother and his wife a break and get Kennedy for the weekend. Allen and Tracey hardly ever call on me to babysit unless it's an emergency or they want to go to dinner or something. Most of the time, I go to their house to see Kennedy, or I will call to see if I can get her for the weekend. I have Kennedy so spoiled; she will cry for me as I'm leaving and, most of the time, I end up taking her with me. Tracey says Kennedy is my baby because she looks just like me when I was her age. It's almost scary. I look at my baby pictures and we do look very much alike. She loves her Auntie Shay and I love her, too.

So, I decide to go to a girl's birthday party who I knew from my college days at Spelman. She recently relocated to the DC area and we've been in touch for a while now. Melanie and I were close while in college, and had many of the same classes together. The party was at the Hyatt hotel in the ballroom. I arrived, parked and sat in the car for ten minutes, checked my makeup and reached in the backseat for her birthday gift before going inside. I saw some other women get out of their cars with gift bags, so I assumed they were going to Melanie's party as well. As I entered the lobby, I saw a sign that read: *Melanie's Fabulous Birthday Bash! Grand Ballroom, 8th Floor.* I forgot how much of a public figure Melanie was until I was asked for my name by the big muscular security staff guarding the door.

"Shayla Richardson," I say, as he flips through the guest list on his clipboard. He looks annoyed because he is on page 10 looking for my name.

"I'm sorry; I don't see you on here." He looks at me.

"Are you sure?" I stand there with the pretty gift bag in my hand.

He flips through his list again. "Oh, I'm sorry, ma'am, you are on the other section of her list."

"Other section?" I am confused as hell.

"Yeah, Ms. Price has another section of her guest list especially for her Spelman classmates. It's kind of like VIP. You get a silver band instead of a plain paper band. This band allows you free drinks all night and access to the press box section of the party. Ms. Price took care of the bar tab for all of you guys who went to Spelman with her."

"Oh, that is so cool, thanks!" I say, excited.

Damn, Melanie is the shit, huh? Well, she is a sportscaster and well known around here. Millions of people see her face on TV all the time. She's one hell of a journalist, too, and contributes to the sports section of the local paper from time to time.

As I enter the ballroom, there is security everywhere. I mean, every single corner of the room has security near it, including the bar. The room is eloquently decorated, and filled with silver, white and blue balloons. All of the tables have cute little place settings with nameplates for each guest. According to the invitation, dinner is going to be catered and served. The hors d'oeuvres are laid out beautifully—little egg rolls, veggies, fruit, cheese and crackers, all sorts of wings, and spinach dip… yummm! I love spinach dip. As my eyes browse the room, I spot several basketball and football players, as well as well-known radio and TV personalities. Melanie is well connected and she knows lots of celebrities. The DJ is cranking, too. This place is awesome. I spot the gift table and place Melanie's gift on the table with the others. I also spot one of my favorite Washington Wizards players, and I want to speak to him, but I really don't have the nerve, so I just admire him from a distance.

"Ma'am, may I take your picture?" a tall handsome gentleman asks me.

"Sure." I strike a pose. Damn, I'm starting to feel like I'm a celebrity now. Wow, Melanie has made every effort to impress for this party—a professional photographer and everything, and a nice looking one, too!

This brother enters the room and his swagger is so damn smooth! It is unbelievable how he has my attention. He's with a friend and I can tell by looking at him and his swag that he has money. I try to avoid those types, but he is a handsome man, that was for sure. He probably is one of Melanie's colleagues or a professional athlete. He is dressed very nicely. Well groomed, wearing huge diamond studs in each ear. His friend is cute, too. I watch them greet a couple of people and make their way to the bar for a drink. This is my chance to make my move and strike up a conversation with him. I approach to the bar, innocently, and order my favorite drink—Pomegranate Martini. A young lady has caught his friend's eye, so he makes his way toward her, already macking on her. I take a sip of my drink, as he orders a Scotch neat. Our eyes lock and he stares at me for a little bit before he says anything. He is making his way over to the other end of the bar area, and I am praying I won't sound like a blubbering idiot! I can't stand that about myself. It's as if I don't know how to have a decent conversation with a man without sounding like a complete idiot. I get nervous and start sweating and stuttering. It's awful, and the more attractive he is, the worse it is. It's sad, too. When I see someone as attractive as this guy, it's as if I already have it in my head that I could never have a chance with someone like him. I really need to work on my self-esteem. When someone tells me I'm cute or pretty, I have a hard time believing them, or have a "yeah right" attitude.

"Why are you at the end of the bar drinking all by yourself?" he says in a sexy voice.

"Oh, I just got here, so I was just checking things out," I say calmly. I seem to be doing okay so far.

"By the way, I'm Jason. I work with Melanie," he says, extending his hand.

"It's nice to meet you, Jason." I shake his hand. "Melanie and I went to college together."

"Is that right?" He sounds surprised.

"Yep, sure is. I've known her for quite a while."

"Yeah, she's cool people," he says, looking into my eyes. "Hey, I didn't catch your name."

"I'm sorry, it's umm, it's Shayla," I say nervously, taking a drink of my martini to try to calm my nerves. Oh gosh, it is happening! I hope I don't screw this up.

"Shayla, what do you do?"

"Oh, I'm a…umm, a business analyst for a software company, specializing in education software." I stumble over every other word. I am having such a hard time carrying on a conversation with him. I don't know why I can't seem to articulate very well what I do for a living. It's really strange.

"Sounds really interesting; you get a little taste of the business side as well as the information technology portion of it. Tell me more."

Oh damn, now why did he have to ask for more? "Well, we umm…" I stop for a minute and take a deep breath, and after I finish exhaling, I press my lips together as I gather my thoughts. I could feel myself getting more and more nervous, and it doesn't help that he is staring me dead in my face, waiting for my response.

"By "we," I mean the business analysts. The group I work with analyzes new and existing education software projects from the programmers and developers. It can get a little stressful at times, but for the most part, I love it." Woo, glad I got through that part.

I am impressed by how interested he is in my career, and he is really a nice guy. I am enjoying my chat with him.

"That's excellent, Shayla. It's always a blessing when you can go to work every day loving what you do."

"Thanks, Jason. Tell me about your job."

"Well, as I said before, I work with Melanie, so I am a sportscaster. I enjoy meeting all the professional athletes and interviewing them. I also enjoy debating the stats and critiquing the players with the other sportscasters while we are live. We have a blast!"

"Wow, sounds like it," I say, with a light chuckle.

Just as I was starting to get comfortable with him and talk without stuttering, I catch a woman staring at us from across the room. This isn't just a curious stare either. Her eyes are really glued on us. It is actually creepy. I saw her a while ago, all up on some football player, and it looked like the poor guy was trying to get away from her. I guess her overflowing breasts and short dress were not enough to keep his attention. She was seriously trying to kick some game to him, too, but he wasn't having it. I could tell he was trying to be as polite as he could. She finally stops staring at us and makes her way over here. She looks like some groupie chick. You know the type, the kind of woman that hangs around at all the parties and knows everything there is to know about all the well-known celebrities in the area. The kind that is damn near a stalker. She seems to know who he is and from what I can tell, she is interested in him.

"Jason darling, there you are. I've been looking all over for you," she says, slinging her weave and looking at him seductively. She acts as if I wasn't even standing there. What a bitch!

"You were looking for me?" he says confused. It's apparent he has no idea who this woman is. It took everything in me not to laugh my ass off.

"Yes silly, you!" She gives me a dirty look, looks me up and down and says, "Will you excuse us, please?"

"Sure," I say, as I press my lips together, still trying to hold my composure. I can't believe some groupie chick is able to just come over and whisk him away like that. I sit at the bar and continue to enjoy my drink. The groupie chick straightens her posture so her breasts are more noticeable to Jason. As she walks away with him, I laugh to myself. The bartender couldn't help but hear me and he laughs, too.

"I have been watching that chick work the room all night. She is determined to land herself somebody with some money tonight. You need another Pomegranate, hun?" he says, still chuckling a little bit.

"Yes please, and by the way, who is that woman anyway, and how did she get in? This party is invitation only. I think Melanie would be pissed if she knew what was going on."

"Yeah, I agree," says the bartender. I'm not sure whom she is, but she has been working this room, that's for sure. Groupies always find a way to get in these types of parties."

He makes me a fresh Pomegranate Martini.

"Thank you so much," I say, leaving him a five-dollar tip on the bar. "I needed this second drink."

"No problem, hun, and thank you."

I think it is time to venture out and find Melanie. I know she is somewhere amongst the large crowd of people. The party has really started to pick up and more people are starting to arrive. I make my way through the crowd, looking for her. I can't find her anywhere, so I figure she must be in the VIP room or something. I show the security guard my wristband and he lets me into the VIP room. I browse the area and there are no signs of Melanie. Hmm... I must have missed her somehow in the main room. The VIP room is very nice. It is an intimate area complete with its own staff, hors d'oeuvres table, and bar. There are even a few couches and a pool table. Just as I sit down, Melanie walks in. She sees me and runs over to me.

"Hey, girl!" I'm so happy to see you. I'm glad you could make it," she says enthusiastically.

"Melanie, you have not changed one bit, girl. Thank you so much for inviting me."

She looks at me, frowns a little and says, "Girl, you know I would not have a party in the DC area without inviting you! You are my girl, and if it weren't for you, I would have flunked statistics and all the math classes for that matter, because I didn't understand any of that crap in college." We both burst into laughter. "Are you having a good time? Did you meet anybody famous yet?"

"Yeah, I'm having a great time, and I think I have met one famous person named Jason."

"Oh girl, you talking about my co-worker, Jason Langley?"

"Yep, that's him. He did say he worked with you. I told him a little about our Spelman days!"

"You did? I hope you didn't tell him that story about my twenty-second birthday, when y'all took me to that club in Atlanta. I thought I was grown and did all them tequila shots and got really messed up. Oh, my gosh, what a night that was."

"Melanie, you are so crazy. I didn't tell him about that."

"Good! It would have ruined my good girl image in the studio."

"Yeah whatever!"

"Come on out here, I want to introduce you to some people." She grabs my hand.

All of a sudden, we don't have to fight the crowds anymore. The security staff outside of the VIP room signals for the crowd to make way for her to walk through. Melanie is getting mad respect. People move out of our way, allowing us to walk through. Besides, it is her party.

Bianca's Thoughts:

Don't be defeated by one bad experience with a man. If it is meant to be, then it will be obvious to you. Don't feel sorry for yourself because it doesn't work out. Something better WILL come along and you will be thanking yourself later for not settling for less. Like the saying goes, "If you settle for less, then you will end up with less than what you settled for!" Wow, what a powerful and true statement!

Be Yourself

Be yourself, because you shouldn't want to be like anyone else
Be yourself, because God handmade each one of us to be
    unique

Be yourself, because that is what a mate will see in you
Be yourself, because that is who you are

Be yourself, and don't you dare let anyone change you
Be yourself, because that's what will attract someone to you

Be yourself, because it's not worth it to be anything less
Be yourself, because after all, you deserve the best

Chapter Seven

ENOUGH ALREADY!

Ashley is on her way over here to borrow an outfit. She has a date with one of her loser boyfriends. I can't keep track with that girl. There's always a different one every couple of months. I am in the kitchen pouring myself a glass of wine and I hear a banging on my door. I know it is her, so I make her wait a few minutes so she could knock like someone with some sense.

I can't believe the nerve of this girl. My little sister is truly a pain in the ass. She comes over to my place to borrow an outfit, but to insult me at the same time. In her opinion, I'm a little old fashioned, so almost every time I see her, she has something negative to say about my hair, clothes, shoes, something! It's actually been this way since we were kids. Mom used to always fuss at us and tell us to shut up the bickering and noise before she beat both our asses. I recall a time when we were teenagers and she always rolled her eyes at me without getting caught. Of course, I would be the one getting caught as I rolled them back.

She would get away with more than Allen and I, being she was the youngest.

"*Mom!*" I screamed down the stairs, "can you make Ashley get out of my room?"

"I'm not even in her stupid room. You make me sick, always tellin' on people," she had said, smacking her teeth at me.

My mom had really had enough of us that day, so I knew somebody was getting their ass beat. I hoped it wasn't going to me. The sound of my mom's footsteps got my heart racing, and Ashley was enjoying the fact that I was scared.

"What is going on up here?" My mom placed her hands on her hips and looked at us for answers.

We were standing in the hallway outside of our bedrooms. Allen was in his room snickering at us as we were scolded by our mother. His room was at the other end of the hall, but he could still hear what was going on.

"Mom, she won't—" we both said, trying to get our mom to listen to us at the same time.

"One at a time, girls," she said, shaking her head, obviously becoming frustrated with us.

"Mom, she has her own room, why does she always have to be in my room trying to be nosey and messing up my stuff?"

Ashley began her famous performance of crying and carrying on. "I don't know why Shayla hates me so much, Mom. I'm just trying to be a good little sister to her. I don't mean any harm."

As soon as she got her last word out, the drama queen broke down crying as if I had really done something wrong to her. She was really performing. I just wanted her to get the fuck out of my room and go back to hers.

"Ashley, stop crying, girl! Shayla does not hate you and you know it. Look, I'm going to say this to both of you. Ask for permission before you go in anybody's bedroom in this house, you understand me?"

"Yes, ma'am," we both said in unison.

"And if I gotta come back up here any more today, I don't care whose fault it is, you both are getting your asses beat! Do not try me. I'm not playing. I'm really sick of all this nonsense between you two. You are sisters for God's sake. You need to learn how to get along!"

My mother went back downstairs and Ashley wiped the tears she had forced out and finally went back to her room.

Boom, boom, boom, boom, boom!

The knocks are louder. One would think she would be knocking more quietly by now, but I forget this is Ashley! I answered the door with my wine in my hand.

"Damn, girl, are you deaf, or are you that tipsy that you didn't hear me knocking?"

"I'm neither, thank you very much," I say sarcastically.

Ashley comes in and heads straight to the kitchen and pours herself a glass of wine.

"Damn, Ashley, won't you have a glass of wine, will ya?"

"What the hell?" she says, frowning at me. "Why are you so damn smart mouthed today, sis?"

"Ashley, I'm really trying to relax this evening. Can you just go on upstairs and pick out an outfit already?"

"Okay!" Her grey eyes study me as if she is trying to figure out my mood. She ran up the stairs and it seems like she has been up there for thirty minutes or more.

I wonder what insults she would have for me today. As I'm going to the kitchen to get a second glass of wine, I hear her stomping down my steps. She appears to be in a big hurry.

"Shayla, this is a wonderful outfit, but you know what?"

I take a deep breath before I answer her. "What Ashley?"

"You should let me go ahead and keep this one," she says, admiring the way the short, pleated, plaid skirt and form-fitting sweater clings to her.

"And, why in the hell would I want to do that?"

"Well, don't take this the wrong way, sis, but do you see how nicely this sweater fits me? This is the way it's supposed to fit," she said arrogantly as she straightened her posture a little.

I turn my head slowly to look her dead in her eyes! "What the hell is that supposed to mean?"

"Girl, you don't have enough breasts to fill out this damn sweater, so it doesn't look right on you. You're too flat for it."

I can't believe the nerve of this bitch! I already wasn't in a very good mood today, and I really don't feel like putting up with her shit. Today is really the wrong day for her to be fucking with me like this. I have way too much patience for this girl now. One of these days, I'm really going to lose it with her, and today might just be the day.

"If you don't like my shit, then take it the fuck off and put it back in my closet! You have a lot of damn nerve coming up in my house, borrowing my shit and then insulting me. Insulting people is just as easy for you as breathing. You really need to think before you speak."

"Sis, I didn't mean to—"

"Mean to what? Insult me once again? You never miss an opportunity to throw an insult at me, do you, Ashley?"

With a shocked expression, her eyes grew wide. I think I was actually scaring her. She had never really seen me like this before. I'm the kind of person who holds stuff in for a long time and I do take a lot of shit, but when I get tired of it, I just explode, and most of the time, what I say ends up coming out the wrong way.

"Ashley, we are not teenagers anymore and Mom is not standing in my living room protecting you. I think you better get the hell out of here before I knock your ass out!"

There is nothing she could say. She just stands there silent, and in amazement. She picks up her purse off the couch and leaves quickly and quietly. I really don't get this girl. I've known her my whole life, so you would think I would be used to it by now, but getting insulted is something you really never get used to. You shouldn't have to get used to something like that especially from your own sister. It really bothers me every time she does it, and I just can't take any more. I start to call her on her cell and apologize, but I change my mind. She deserved that shit. I wonder how long it will be before she starts in on me again.

Ashley waited nervously for her date to arrive. They were to meet at this nice sushi bar downtown DC. She met Travis at a club about a month ago. They have been dating for a few weeks. There is only one problem with Travis. He can't satisfy her sexually and she is bored already with their sex life. Why can't most pretty boys put it down in the bedroom? Travis was fine! He stood six-foot-three inches tall, and weighed about two hundred and five pounds. He was built like a basketball player. He worked for the federal government downtown. He never talked about his job too much. What he did talk about a lot though was his ex-wife. He has been divorced for about three years now and Ashley has noticed he talks about her way too much, which really annoyed the shit out of her. Travis came rushing through the door and approached the table.

"Sorry I'm late, baby, got held up in traffic," he said, kissing her cheek gently.

"Oh it's cool, how are you?"

"Pretty good, pretty good," he said taking his seat.

"I ordered wine for us, I hope it's okay."

"It's fine, honey," he said, taking her hands into his. He stared at her for a few seconds as if something was on his mind. He took a deep breath before he began to vent. "Can you believe that trick is trying to take my dog away?"

"What trick?"

"Who else! That damn Anita" he said, obviously frustrated. "I'm not giving her the dog after all this time."

Ashley tried to put on the best smile she could without showing her disgust. They had been divorced for three years. Why couldn't he stop talking about that woman? Nothing tied them together except that damn dog! They didn't have any children together, so there was no reason for them to be in constant contact with each other. Ashley was starting to think they were still fucking!

The first week she met Travis, he spent two hours talking about that woman. How she did him wrong by cheating on him and how much of a ho she was. He didn't have anything nice to say about her, and she didn't particularly care for all ex-wife bashing either. Quite frankly, it was a turn off. Although what the ex-wife did was wrong, she didn't need to hear about it every other day. Enough was enough. She took a deep breath as she tried to console him.

"Why don't you take a couple of deep breaths and calm down."

"I'm really trying to, Ashley, but this woman is always trying to pull some shit to make my life hell. I gave her a very generous divorce settlement that included the house, one of the cars, and some mutual funds. Nothing was ever brought up about Jordie, and now all of a sudden, she wants her. There's not a chance in hell she's getting her. Nope, not gonna let it happen."

Ashley was in disbelief. They were arguing over a damn dog! She realized the aftermath of a divorce could be messy, but that was just ridiculous.

"Let's order, shall we?" she said, attempting to change the subject.

Travis was still very annoyed. It was almost like he didn't even hear what she said. He leaned back in his chair and shook his head.

"I guess I have to call my lawyer tomorrow and file papers to keep Jordie. I had her long before Anita and I even got together."

Ashley was pissed off now. He was ruining their evening with that ex-wife talk. A waiter walked by and she got his attention.

"Excuse me, can you tell me your specials for this evening?"

"Sure ma'am, your waiter is Tommy. I will send him over right away."

"Thanks." She took a deep breath. At that point, she was the one who needed to calm down, because she was two seconds from walking out of here.

A couple minutes later, Tommy came over to explain all the specials they had for the evening. The restaurant had an elaborate sushi menu, and she wanted to try something different. She ordered the California roll, and Travis ordered the vegetarian maki. Travis wasn't really a meat eater. He was a borderline vegetarian. He probably ate meat once a week.

Their meals came and they enjoyed their sushi. Surprisingly, Anita's name didn't come up anymore during their meal. Ashley was very happy about that, however, it did kind of ruin the mood for her. She had planned on giving him some after they left, but all that talk about Anita before killed that. As they were leaving the restaurant heading for the car, Travis began to get a little flirty. He brushed up against her curves with an erect penis.

"You feel that? It's ready for you," he said seductively.

Ashley felt his hardness up against her, but she was not in the mood, not tonight.

"I have a really early class tomorrow, Travis, so I'm going to have to give you a rain check okay."

"Rain check? What the hell?" He seemed confused.

"Sorry, this is the last class before finals, so I really need to be there. I am in law school you know."

"I know, sweetie, but I want you *so* bad." His breath now breathing on her neck and his hand now under her skirt. Their lips met, and she kissed him passionately. People were walking by, looking at them, as they entered the restaurant.

"Travis, we have to stop, people are starting to stare."

"I don't care, let 'em look."

She gave him one last gentle kiss on the lips and he looked into her eyes and said, "Okay, I understand. Let me walk you to your car."

As soon as they arrived across the parking lot to Ashley's car, a silver BMW 7 series pulled into one of the parking spaces. Out of nowhere, Travis says, with excitement, "Wow, that's a nice car! That's the kind of car Anita wants."

Ashley cut her eyes at him and said, "That's nice," in a very annoying tone. "I'll talk to you later, Travis."

"Okay honey, I'll call you."

Ashley headed toward Pennsylvania Avenue, enjoying the night air. She couldn't believe the nerve of Travis. Something definitely is still going on between him and that woman. She knew this for a fact because of something she had found prior to their dinner that night. Not only that, but you don't let anyone get under your skin like that for nothing, especially if you have supposedly moved on. Ashley thought back to a time when she was at Travis' house and he had fallen asleep. Being the inquisitive person that she is, she went through his phone. It was sitting there on the night stand and she figured Travis wasn't going to wake up anytime soon. He was already snoring anyway. His phone was a little different than hers, so it took her a couple minutes to figure out how everything worked. The only thing she really wanted to see his call log and text messages. His phone did not have email capability, but she wished it did. She could have seen a lot of stuff that way. She first scrolled through the call log where she saw her name listed several times. They talked quite a bit during the day, so that didn't surprise her. Next, she saw his brother's number and he was listed as many times as she was. A lot of strange names were also listed that she had never heard him bring up before, but she didn't really worry about that too much because she had not been dating him that long. There were several women listed in his call log though, and she wasn't sure how she felt about that.

Now it was time for her to start looking through the text messages. She started with the outbox so she could see some of the things he was saying. He had responded to some women with casual responses like "HEY WHAT'S UP," or "JUST CHILLIN," so she kept looking. Then she saw something that looked really interesting. Now Travis had been sweatin' her for a while now and she wouldn't give him the time of day at first. Then one night she saw him out at a club and he convinced her to go out with him. He claimed to be so single and unattached, so why in the world is he sending a few women "I LOVE YOU" and "I MISS YOU" text messages? She didn't know, but she was determined to find out. She needed to investigate further so she moved on to the inbox. What she found was shocking. Some messages were sent from a woman named Tammy saying she missed him. She sent those a lot from what Ashley could see. There was also a couple from a woman named Renee who said she missed him and she seemed to send him messages every day with her daily activities. These looked like "check in" messages. What shocked her most though is what she found next. There were several text messages from Anita. The ex-wife he claims is so evil and he can't stand. Now she knows where the "I love you" texts came from. Anita sent him messages every single morning. Sometimes they were innocent messages, sometimes they were those romantic, lovey dovey type messages, and he definitely responded with something romantic as well as he did with the other women. Most of his responses were warm and romantic to them all. Now she was really starting to put the pieces together. Not only were Travis and Anita still in love and seeing each other, but Mr. Travis was obviously a player and a big damn liar! Ashley later found out their divorce wasn't even final yet. They were still going through stuff in court and fighting over this and that. She thought about how upset he was at dinner that night and how he couldn't stop talking about her. Was he acting? He had to be because it's obvious they both still have feelings for each other. She had seen enough, so she closed the phone and put it back on his nightstand. She was disappointed because she liked him, but lucky for her, she didn't develop any feelings for him yet, so it's a good thing she found out about him early. When they started dating, she felt early on that something wasn't right, so she took her time with him. He seemed a little too eager for her taste. He was trying to rush her into a relationship, but she kept telling him to slow down and that she would not be pressured into something she wasn't ready for. He seemed to understand and backed off from the idea a little. She never saw him or talked to him again after their dinner date that night and she never told him why either. He kept calling her, but she wouldn't return his phone calls. She didn't feel the need to tell him what she had discovered and she sure as hell didn't want to give him the chance to explain anything, or try to talk his way out of it. He has no idea she knows about the text messages.

Men think they are slick! They do little sneaky shit and think they are not going to be caught. They tell you one thing and do another. They look you dead in your face and lie to you by telling you they are single and no longer interested in their exes. Travis will not get the chance to play my sister for a fool like he's doing those other women. A lot of this brother's story wasn't adding up anyway. I am glad it is over. Big lesson learned here ladies! When something doesn't feel right, investigate. Check out his story and keep your eyes and ears open when he's talking. Eventually, he will slip up and make a mistake. You have to protect your heart and prevent hurt if you can. Many times, you can't prevent yourself from getting hurt and stuff like this happens after the fact. Nobody wants to be played for a fool, so if you see warning signs early, get out of it!

Bianca's Thoughts:

Really, dude? You talk about your ex that much? Wow! If anyone talks about his or her ex that much around you, then you need to rethink why you are even around this person. If they have to talk about their ex that much, then there are obviously some unresolved or lingering feelings on their part. How annoying and disrespectful is that? That would make me feel uncomfortable. Let them go back to their ex!

Chapter Eight

WE ALL GOT ISSUES!

Morning came too early for me, especially since today is Saturday and I usually sleep in on the weekends. I stared at the clock and it read 9:05. I turned over and attempted to fall back asleep, but the phone ringing ruined any chance of that happening. I looked at the caller ID and it was a damn telemarketer! I hate telemarketers. They always seem to call at the worst times. *Why the hell do they call so early on the weekends?* I was in no mood to hear anyone's sales pitch, but I couldn't stand the sound of the phone constantly ringing so I picked it up.

"Hello," I said with an attitude.

"Good morning, may I speak to Mr. or Mrs. Richardson." The woman's voice on the other end of the phone was so pleasant, and I really didn't want to be rude to her, but I didn't feel like this today.

"Neither one of them are here," I lied.

"Okay, when would be a good time to call back," she said pleasantly.

"How about ummm…never!" *CLICK!*

I hung up on her ass. I told y'all I wasn't in the mood. I managed to drift back off for a little bit until the phone started ringing again. *I'll be damned! Another telemarketer. I'm about sick of their asses today!* "STOP FUCKIN CALLING HERE!" I screamed into the phone and slammed it back down. I finally gave up on getting any sleep, so I decided to get up, take a shower, and put some clothes on. I stood in my walk in closet trying to decide what to put on. I grabbed some jeans and put them on. *Now I have to find a shirt.* As my eyes searched the row of neatly folded shirts, I ran across an old picture of me and my ex-boyfriend Jamal from college. I thought I had gotten rid of all of his pictures, but I guess not. This one was tucked away behind some shirts. I stood there in the middle of the closet staring at the picture of us. We were at a New Years Eve party and we looked so happy. I put the picture on the shelf for a second as I picked out a shirt and put it on. I grabbed the picture and held it close to my heart as I walked into my bedroom and sat on the edge of my bed. I looked at the picture again and all of a sudden, tears filled my eyes and I started to cry uncontrollably. It was like all of those old feelings came rushing back, especially the pain from the breakup.

I went to the bathroom to get a tissue and attempted to get myself together. I can't believe that it still hurts, all these years later. Knowing you were the one responsible for ruining your own happiness is a hard pill to swallow and digest. Every day of my life, I regret the fact that I ruined that relationship. When

I look back on how sweet Jamal was to me, I realized I might never find that again.

It's hard to find someone who cares deeply for you, so when you do find that person, you should hold on to them. Man, I screwed that up real bad. I should have never broken up with him. He was so loving toward me. Everyone saw that. I had a lot of issues to work through and I should have taken care of them before entering into a relationship with someone, but I thought I could do both.

I had to get out of the house for a little while. I went down the street to Starbucks to get my favorite vanilla latte. I sat there watching all the people rush in and out, then I saw all the happy couples sitting there looking deeply into each other's eyes. I couldn't help but remember when Jamal and I use to look at each other like that. My mind started to wonder a little. Am I ever going to have something like that again? I think I have been more than patient waiting for Mr. Right. He may not be here in the DC area, who knows. He could be anywhere. While sitting there enjoying my latte, a man approached me and asked me for my phone number. I let him down easy, explaining to him that I was healing from a broken heart, which was half-true. Why does this type of shit always happen to me? I'm always getting approached by guys I'm not interested in, and while I do feel bad for having to turn them down, I also feel like "damn, WTF is wrong with me?" Why wont someone halfway decent looking approach me for a change? On the rare occasion some cute guy does approach me, something always happens. They usually end up being married or have a girlfriend. Sometimes they are too damn busy to make plans with you or even return your damn phone calls. One thing I will never ever do again in my lifetime is chase a man. That is one of the most degrading things you can ever do to yourself. A woman can tell when a man is not interested. If you find yourself in a situation like this, ladies, please keep it moving. Do not continue to pursue the man. Just walk away from it and leave it alone. You will save yourself a lot of heartache; trust me. There are too many men out here in this huge world we live in, so for any woman to waste her time and energy on chasing one man is absolutely ridiculous! Say it with me ladies – **I WILL NEVER CHASE A MAN, I AM BETTER THAN THAT, AND I LOVE MYSELF TOO MUCH TO LET MY SELF ESTEEM BE SHOT DOWN BY SOME MAN WHO DOESN'T GIVE A DAMN ABOUT ME!!**

I went back home and relaxed on the couch, still enjoying what was left of my latte. I turned the TV on to my favorite channel (Lifetime) hoping to catch a good movie. There are always movies on Lifetime on Saturdays. I managed to find a good movie that was just starting, so I curled up on the couch with a blanket and watched it. The sound of the phone ringing annoyed me, and I ignored it for the first couple of rings. *You've got to be kidding me! This better not be a telemarketer.* I looked on the caller ID and it read PRICE, MELANIE.

"Hello"

"Hey, Shayla, it's Melanie"

"Hey, Melanie, what's up, girl?"

"Not too much, girl, what are you doing?"

"Oh nothing really, just watching a movie on Lifetime."

"Girl, that sounds so relaxing. She said with a chuckle. I was wondering if you wanted to meet up for lunch later on."

"Sure, what are you in the mood for?"

"It doesn't matter. You know I'm not picky. The girls are gone with their dad this weekend, so I figure I better take advantage of this free time I have you know."

"Okay, well let's meet up around 12:30 at Applebee's, is that alright?"

"Yep, I'll see you then, Shayla."

"Okay, bye."

A lunch outing with my girl from college sounds nice right about now. Melanie didn't quite sound like herself. It was almost as if she had something on her mind. I hope she's okay. I know she just got back into the area not long ago, so I figured she would be still catching up with most of us. I locked up the house and headed for Applebee's to meet Melanie. I looked for her as I walked in, but I didn't see her, so I decided to stand in the lobby and wait for her. Five minutes later, I looked out the window, and there she was, stepping out of her dark grey BMW 760. *Damn! That's a $70,000 car. I wish I could afford a ride like that! That thing is nice!* She walked in kind of in a hurry.

"Hey Shayla, sorry I'm running late girl" she said sticking her gloves into her pockets.

"Oh girl, it's alright. I've only been here a few minutes."

All of a sudden, this perky little star struck hostess greeted us.

"Oh my gosh! It's her, y'all, it's Melanie Price!" said the hostess. She was so star struck; I couldn't believe what I was witnessing right now. Melanie looked so calm and she was just smiling. She probably gets this kind of treatment all the time. By now, nearly the whole Applebee's staff was out there in the lobby with us with their cell phones taking pictures of Melanie.

"Melanie, you are the bomb girl! You are my favorite sportscaster, and you're black! I'm so proud of that, I mean, how many Black female sportscasters are on TV right now, maybe one or two?" said the hostess. Her rambling was starting to get on my nerves now and I was hungry!

"What's your name?" said Melanie

"Oh, please forgive me for going on and on like that, I'm Stella"

"Stella, it is so good to meet you"

"Is this your sister?"

"No, said Melanie with a chuckle. This is my good friend from college, Shayla"

"Nice to meet you Shayla" she said still full of excitement"

"It's good to meet you too Stella," I said, shaking her hand.

"May, I take a picture with the both of you?"

"Sure, if it's okay with you Shayla?"

"Yeah, sure!" I said, surprised. She handed her camera to one of her co-workers and they took the picture of us.

"Thank you so much, Melanie," she said, looking like she was about to burst.

"You're welcome," said Melanie.

"Your table is right this way," she said, as we followed her to the other side of the restaurant. "Your server will be right with you."

"Thank you," said Melanie.

We settled into our booth and our server came over. Luckily, she wasn't star struck at all like the hostess. I'm sure she knew who Melanie was, but she was just trying to be professional and do her job.

"Good afternoon, ladies, my name is Tia and I will be taking care of you today. Can I get you started with something to drink?"

"I'll have a margarita please," I said, still examining the menu.

"Hmm… so many drink choices to choose from," said Melanie. I'll have a margarita as well."

"Alright, I will put those in for you and be back shortly with your drinks ladies," said the server walking away.

"Thanks," I said with a smile.

Tia was really a nice server and I could already tell she was going to get a fat tip!

"So, Melanie, catch me up on what's been going on with you. I haven't had the chance to catch up with you since you got back from LA," I said.

"Well, Shay, a lot has happened since the last time we talked girl. You know I have two daughters right?"

"Yeah, I remember you mentioning that the last time I called. Are you and their dad still together?" I inquired.

Melanie lowered her head and went silent for a moment. She pressed her lips together and shook her head no. When she raised her head, her eyes were full of tears.

"Oh Melanie, honey, what happened?"

Before she began to speak, Tia came back with our drinks.

"Here you are ladies, two margaritas," Tia said as she sat each of our drinks down in front of us.

"Thanks," I said, putting my focus back on Melanie's sad face. I was getting really worried about her right now.

"Well, first of all let me just say this up front, Derek is a wonderful father to my girls. He really loves them and would do anything for them. I guess he and I were just on two different paths. We were together for a long time, about six years. A lot of you at school didn't know this, but I was pregnant with Nia when I graduated. I didn't want anyone to know, especially my parents because they would have hit the roof. Derek and I kept it a secret, no one knew except him and me. After graduation, he convinced me to move to LA. His schedule was crazy, you know, with him being a professional athlete and all; it was hard for him to keep flying back and forth to Atlanta. He bought me this huge beautiful condominium in LA, which I still own, and shortly after that Nia was born. I still had not found a job yet, but I had some good leads from the internship I had done in Atlanta after graduation. My not working was perfectly fine with Derek, because he didn't want me to work anyway. He wanted me to focus on being a mom to Nia. He had also hired a nanny, which we didn't need since I wasn't working, but he insisted on us having one. I didn't want for anything. He took good care of us and handled everything. We were doing well and we were happy together, so a couple years later, we had Deren. Nia was named after me, and Deren after him. We had fun coming up with those names. Girl, I'm telling you this brotha's game was so smooth! You not gonna believe what happened next. I was doing the girls laundry one day, and a pair of his jeans ended up at the bottom of their hamper. I think he must have put them in there by accident or something. Anyways, when I was separating the clothes, there was this piece of paper sticking out of one of the pockets. When I opened it, I was confused. It was a mortgage statement for a home in San Diego a few hours from where we lived. So, me, being the detective that I am, started to immediately do some research online. Well, it didn't take a genius to put that together from there, right?"

"Oh my gosh, girl! I said in shock. His ass is married?"

"Yeah, was married. He's divorced now, but he was married the entire time we were together. Living a double life! I don't know how he pulled it off, because he was with us 90% of the time. The rest of that time was spent on the road at away games."

"Melanie, I am so sorry. What did you do next?"

Before she could answer, Tia came back to take our orders. I ordered the grill chicken salad and Melanie ordered the chicken enchiladas. She continued with her story.

"Girl, I was so hurt, I couldn't even think straight. I didn't want to believe it at first, but I kept doing my research and found out he was indeed married. I even called to their house and pretended to be a sales person trying to sell them stuff. He was there a couple of times, but most of the time she was there alone. They don't have any children together, thank God, but he had to pay her a lot of money in their divorce settlement. When I confronted him, he was real smooth and calm. Of course, he denied it at first, and kept denying it for quite a while. I guess once he realized I was done with him, he came clean about it. He gave me some bullshit about them not really being together anymore, but just living under the same roof. I didn't believe him at all. All I knew was that I wasn't going to have any part in that drama and refused to be the other woman. He tried to get me back for a long time but it didn't work. He finally moved out of our condominium as well as his other place with his wife and signed over full ownership of the place to me. I had to leave LA, so I took my girls and came back home to DC. Nobody knew I was here for the first year, except Derek. I didn't want my family in my business. I went through a bad period of depression, and being a single mom as well as being famous was starting to stress me out badly. My relief finally came when Derek divorced his wife and followed me to DC to be closer to the girls. He keeps them on Tuesdays and every single weekend. He is an amazing dad; I won't take that from him. He was just a lousy boyfriend!"

Tia came with our food, and we blessed it and began to eat some of it.

"Melanie, this is so wild! I can't believe Derek was married the whole time. People can really fool you if they try hard enough. I wonder how long would he have kept up the charade if you had not caught him."

I sat there in disbelief as we ate our lunch. Melanie confided in me that the relationship almost took her life and she had no will to live at one point. She was severely depressed for quite some time. She even had to take a leave of absence from her job. She also said she would never date another famous person again because she had dangerous experiences with their groupies. Derek bought her a BMW X5 truck shortly after their youngest daughter was born because he knew she would need a bigger vehicle that would accommodate their two small children. A groupie flattened all four tires one day while she was at the mall shopping. When she got to the parking lot, a cop had caught the chick in the act and he was in the process of arresting her. As the cop was shoving her into the police car, the woman was shouting all kinds of things at Melanie like "Your man got some good dick, girl, I see why you are holding on to him" and "He really knows how to use that tongue, too!" She really didn't know what to believe because some of these girls were truly crazy and some of them were just aggressive and went after what they wanted.

"So, how are you and Derek getting along now? How are the girls coping?" I asked.

"Derek and I are good now because it's been a couple years since I've been back. The girls have adjusted really well to the situation. At first, I couldn't even look at him, but since we have children together, I had to see him sometime. Most of the time when he came to pick up the kids, I would ask my nanny to take them down to the lobby to meet him because I just couldn't do it all the time. Now, it's cool. He comes up to get them and drop them back off and there are no issues. I think I have finally healed over the whole situation and am finally ready to start dating again. I thought I would never get to that point, because Derek crushed many of my dreams. I thought he was going to be the one I married and would be the father of all of my children. I've always wanted a large family, so we were planning to have a couple more kids. I guess that won't be happening now, at least not with him. Every now and then, he still tries to test me to see where my feelings are for him, but the truth of the matter is I feel absolutely nothing for him. He killed all of my feelings I had for him. He could never come back into my life romantically, not EVER!"

"I don't blame you at all, Melanie. You have to protect your heart and do what you have to do. If you ever need any help with the girls or anything, just let me know, I'm here for you girl," I said.

"Aww, thank you, Shayla!" she said, placing her hand over her chest. "I may take you up on that one day. Are you sure you can handle a five- and seven-year-old? You know you can come get them for practice because it will be your turn one day."

"Girl, please, I can handle them! I keep my niece Kennedy all the time."

"Okay, I'm going to remember that," she said raising her eyebrows. Kids can be a lot of work. I'm very blessed to have the nanny on call to help me out because my schedule can be crazy at times. My nanny is not a live in though because I want to raise my own kids, not have a nanny do it. Normally, I have to be at the studio at 6a.m. to tape the show, so she will come in the morning around 5a.m. and get them off to school for me around 8:00. I do the sports highlights from the NBA games that came on the day before and sometimes I will hang around the studio to do some additional commentary if they need me too. Most days, I am out of there by 1:00, so I have plenty of time to pick up the girls from school at 3:30. Derek insists on the kids attending private school because of our jobs, so he covers the cost of that."

"Girl, your schedule sounds pretty good, but manageable," I said, taking another bite of my salad.

"Yeah, it is for the most part. It gets a little crazy around finals though," she said.

We finished our meals and enjoyed the rest of our margaritas.

"Shayla, thanks so much for meeting me for lunch and for listening."

"No problem, girl! Anytime! That's what friends are for," I said.

Tia came to the table with our check and as I reached for my debit card, Melanie put her hand up and said "Lunch is on me Shayla."

"Oh, thanks Melanie, that's nice of you."

She took care of the bill and we walked out of Applebee's. As we were walking out of the restaurant, people were staring and snapping pictures of Melanie. I gave her a hug as she got into her car.

"Call me if you need me, okay Melanie? I'm serious. If you need to talk, you know how to get in touch with me."

"Okay, Shayla, I will," she said.

I got in my car and headed to Allen and Tracey's house to see Kennedy. All that talk about kids made me miss my little niece a little bit. Melanie's story really shocked me and got me thinking. You never know what a person is going through just by looking at them. Now the average person would probably guess Melanie has this fabulous, happy life because she's on TV, but in reality, she doesn't. She's still hurting on the inside, I can tell because I've been there. She is a strong woman though and I admire her for the way she's handling this. She is staying strong for her kids and they are what are keeping her going. She is really a good person and deserves to be happy. I was so glad to hear she's ready to start dating again. Any man would be blessed to have her in their life. She's such a warm, compassionate person. I'm glad her and I got a chance to catch up because it really has been a long time since we spoke, at least over a year I believe.

Bianca's Thoughts:

Just because a person has money doesn't mean they are happy. A person looking at her situation from the outside will probably say Melanie should be happy because she is very fortunate and has money, right? Wrong! People shouldn't assume a person is happy based on appearance. You never know what's going on inside of that person. Everyone is fighting some sort of battle.

5 Months

5 months had went by since the last time I spoke to him
His phone call surprised me, that voice still gentle as a gem
A love that strong is really hard to forget...
And although I tried, deep down I knew I didn't want to quit

Right now I can't really describe what I'm feeling
No pain or sadness though, but potential healing
Healing from all the guilt that I've been carrying around
For breaking up with him, he didn't make a sound

I hope he knows how sorry I am for the pain that I caused
I know I really hurt him and because of that, our lives took a
    pause
Can you please forgive me for doing that? This I really need to
    know
I've been depressed about it for quite a while, and trying not to
    let it show

This love I have for him, I don't want to share it with no one else
Others have tried to approach me, but I wasn't even about to fool
    myself
Fool myself into believing I could ever love someone else that
    way again
I was not about to lie to myself or even try to pretend

Is He All That?

He did something for me that nobody else has been able to do
He broke down that wall and all my insecurities, he got me
    through
I didn't believe love would ever happen like that for me
But I was wrong and later on, I began to see

Our conversations lately have been very nice and loving
My fondest memories are of us just looking at the water and
    hugging
This is truly and honestly the greatest love I've ever had
It's time to be happy again, no more being sad

Chapter Nine

WHAT'S DONE IN THE DARK...

I arrived at my brother's house and it looks like nobody is home. I rang the doorbell. No answer. I rang it again and I hear someone running up the stairs. Finally, Allen comes to the door sweating and out of breath.

"Hey sis," he says, out of breath. Come on in."

"Man, what are you doing?" I said with a laugh.

"I was just finishing up my workout downstairs."

"Oh, I'm sorry, I didn't mean to interrupt. I just dropped by to see Kennedy."

"She's next door playing with her little friend, but I will go get her. I'm sure she'll be happy to see you as always."

"Where's Tracey?" I asked.

"Oh, she went out to lunch with one of her friends," said Allen.

"Looks like we had the same idea today, because I just got back from lunch with Melanie."

"Melanie?" He was shocked. "The same Melanie you went to college with and who's now on TV?"

"Yep!"

"Man, I haven't seen her since your college graduation. Well, other than on TV. Umm... I'd like to get ahold of her and...."

"ALLEN! I yelled at him. You are married, you better cut that out!"

"I know girl, I'm just playing! But she is fine as hell though."

I shook my head at him as he walked out the door to go get Kennedy. Two minutes later Kennedy comes rushing through the door and she was running full speed ahead right at me.

"Auntie Shay, Auntie Shay!" she said jumping into my arms.

"Hey there, how is Auntie's baby."

"I'm good! Can I go with you Auntie, please, can I," she said, squeezing me with a tight hug.

Allen just stood there in amazement. He couldn't believe how attached his daughter was to me and he knew she was going to have her way, because I just could not say no to this little girl. She has me completely wrapped around her finger. I don't know what's going to happen when I start having my own kids. I'm the only Aunt she see's because Ashley is too irresponsible to watch anyone's kids or spend time with them, so Kennedy rarely sees her. She's not a "kid" person. She's too busy anyway with law school and all.

"So, is it safe to assume you will be bringing her back tomorrow sometime sis?"

"Yeah, you know the drill, I said shaking my head. I hope Tracey doesn't mind."

"Nah, it's cool, he said. I'm sure she would welcome the break.

Kennedy got her favorite doll and we were on our way back to my place. It was still early in the day, so I decided to take her for ice cream. When we were pulling up in the parking lot, we could see a lot of people sitting outside of the ice cream shop enjoying their ice cream. It was a nice day for this, so I guess everyone had the same idea. I was about to get out the car, but something caught my eye. I couldn't believe it. *Is that Tracey over there with another dude?* I thought, *Nah, it can't be her!* I got a closer look and, it was her. They were now kissing and he was caressing her face. I was heated! My poor brother! Here he is thinking she is out to lunch with one of her girlfriends and she's out here seeing another man! Man, she is so lucky I have Kennedy with me, because I would walk right up on her and bust her because I bet he doesn't know she's married. I sure as hell didn't see that big ass ring my brother bought her on her finger! I just sat there blank. I didn't know what to do with this information. I will deal with her ass later!

"Auntie Shay, are we going to get ice cream now," asked Kennedy.

"Umm yes, sweetheart, but we are going to go to a different place because this one has a long line."

I drove off mad as hell. We ended up at another ice cream place where we sat inside and enjoyed our ice cream. Kennedy was really enjoying herself. She passed out in the car on the way home, which meant she was going to be up all night. After I put her down in the guest room, I ordered some Chinese food so when she woke up there would be something there for her to eat. I normally don't cook on the weekends, so I knew we would be eating out. She didn't stay sleep too long; maybe an hour and she did wake up hungry. I fixed her a plate of shrimp and broccoli, sat at the table, and ate with her. She was such a well-mannered child and very smart for a three year old.

"Auntie Shay, when are we going to paint my room pink?" she asked.

"Your room?"

"Yeah, my room, the one I sleep in all the time when I come here?"

I busted out laughing at her. What a perceptive little girl. She was a mess! I couldn't do nothing but laugh.

"We will have to see about that okay sweetie," I reassured her.

"Okay Auntie."

We finished our meal and parked ourselves in front of the couch to watch a kiddie movie. She was sleeping a couple of hours later, so I took her up to "her" room. I took her home in the morning and I couldn't wait to fuck with Tracey about her "lunch with her girlfriend." I rang the doorbell and she answered.

"Hey baby girl, how's mommy's girl," she said picking Kennedy up.

"Hey Shayla, how's it going?"

"Pretty good," I said, glaring at her as she played the perfect little wife and mother role. She noticed it right away. I could tell by the look in her eye that she knew her ass was in trouble.

"Kennedy, sweetheart, why don't you go and put your things away in your room," she said.

"Okay Mommy. Bye Auntie Shay," Kennedy said as she ran up the stairs.

"Bye baby," I said.

"Shayla, is something wrong?"

"You tell me, Tracey! Was lunch good with your girlfriend the other day, or did you enjoy the ice cream with your piece on the side better?"

Tracey took a deep breath. She couldn't believe what was going on here. She wasn't even going to try to lie her way out of it, because obviously Shayla knew her dirty little secret. No need in making it worse by lying she thought.

"Okay Shayla, what do you know?"

"I know you sneaking around and cheating on my brother."

"Shhh….. girl, keep your voice down. He is home you know," she said with a frown.

"Listen here you little BITCH," I said as low as I could and with as much force as I could. "My brother has been nothing but good to you. Tracey, you don't even have to fuckin' work! You get to stay home and raise your daughter and spend lots of time with her. Allen has been good to you as far as I can see. Now, I don't know what's going on with you, but you better get this shit together and soon, or I'm going to tell him."

"Shayla, please let me explain. You don't understand. The fire is gone in my marriage and I don't know what else to do. Your brother is a wonderful guy, but I really don't think he's the man for me. I'm sorry Shayla, but I'm planning to leave him."

"You gonna leave my brother for that bitch ass nigga I saw you having ice cream with? Oh, hell no! You are a stupid bitch. Do you know how many women, like myself, who are still waiting for a good man to come along? Girl, you don't know how good you have it."

"Call me what you want, but I can't do this much longer, and you don't have to worry about telling him because I plan to do it soon."

"Well let me tell you something Tracey," I said getting in her face. "You got 30 days to tell him about the cheating. If you don't tell him, I will."

A few seconds later, Allen came walking down the hall and we tried to act as normal as possible.

"Hey sis, I didn't hear you come in."

"Hey Allen, I said giving him a hug.

"You two look pretty intense right now. Everything okay in here?"

Tracey and I just looked at each other with fake smiles.

"Everything is fine Allen," I said trying to reassure him. "I'm gonna be late for my kickboxing class and I hate being late. You never know when you are going to have to just kick somebody's ass, so I need to be ready at all times," I said giving Tracey a sly look as I walked out the door.

That stupid bitch, I thought as I drove off. I could have beaten her ass right then and there. She is so lucky my niece and my brother were home, because it would have been on. I'm generally not a violent person at all, but if I'm pushed over the edge, watch out. The little quiet girl named Shayla quickly turns into Sheila, my alter ego! That saying "What's done in the dark will be brought to the light" is so true. Tracey thought she was getting away with something and she wasn't because she was caught. How dumb are you to be a married woman out in public having ice cream with your lover.

Bianca's Thoughts:

Wow! The woman who looks like she has it all is having an affair huh? The question is how long has she been having this affair? You never know because people can hide things like this for a long time and get away with it. You would be surprised how long people actually get away with things like this. Sometimes it goes on for years. It's unbelievable. How do people do this? How do you love two people at the same time? How do you become intimate with two people at the same time? I couldn't do it. My conscious would have gotten the best of me and I would have told on myself within the first month.

Chapter Ten

MOVIN' ON UP

I entered Sam Ford's office nervously. He signaled for me to come in and sit down as he was finishing his phone call with a project manager. He did not seem happy and I was hoping I wasn't there to add to his stress.

"I don't care if you have to work overtime," he said, coming closer to his desk. "That profit analysis better be on my desk by Friday."

The loud sound of him slamming the phone startled me. I've never seen Mr. Ford that upset. I really didn't have much interaction with him at work, only when something was wrong or he had a question about something program specific we were working on. Sam Ford was a tall, thin, Caucasian man with a full beard and slicked back hair. He was always very cordial to me when I saw him in the hallway. His office was on the eighth floor and mine is on the third so I very rarely see him. He is the CFO and works for the President of the company. He collected himself before he spoke.

"Sorry about that, Shayla" he said, leaning back in his chair and loosening one of the buttons on his blazer. "Mr. Jamison has been on me about getting this project out the door."

"That's quite alright," I said, pressing my lips together. He twisted his mouth, took a deep breath and started to massage his chin. He was starting to make me nervous because he seemed like he had something on his mind he needed to tell me but didn't know how.

"Shayla, you've been with us for a couple years now and your performance is outstanding, however, I don't think what you are currently doing is working out for us anymore. I need you to pack up your office by the end of the day."

My eyes started tearing up and my heart started beating very fast because it sounded like I was being fired. What was he saying? OMG, I thought to myself. *What in the world did I do? Was it that run-in with Ron I had a couple months back? I wonder if he filed a complaint against me, or something.* My mind was racing and I didn't know what to think.

"Mr. Ford, I don't understand. What do you mean? Am I being fired?" I asked nervously.

"Fired?" Mr. Ford said as he started laughing uncontrollably.

Oh, geez… he was really making me nervous now! What the hell is going on here? This man just told me to pack up my office and he's laughing his ass off about it.

"No, no Shayla… you aren't fired. You are being replaced by someone," he said.

"I'm confused Mr. Ford. Being fired and replaced is the same thing," I said confused.

"Not in this case Shayla" he said shaking his head. "I'm sorry. I didn't mean to scare you. I should have been clearer. You are being replaced because you are being promoted," he said with a huge smile on his face.

"Woo," I said, breathing a sigh of relief. "Mr. Ford, I thought you were firing me. Oh my goodness, you have no idea how relieved I am. I am being promoted. Wow! But you told me to pack up my office; I'm still a little confused."

"Shayla, you are being promoted from business analyst to project manager, and you are going to have to pack up your office because you are moving to the eighth floor."

"Mr. Ford, I don't know what to say," I said anxiously. "Thank you so much for this opportunity. It's really an honor that you are giving me this job after only being with the company for two years."

"Well Shayla, we normally wait to promote analysts to project managers after they have been in their current position for three years. The requirements for this job may seem a bit overwhelming to you at first, but trust me you can handle it. You are ready. Mr. Jamison and I were discussing you the other day. You have exceeded our expectations in such a short time, so we felt it was time to promote you. We've only done this for two employees, and you will be working with them. They are project managers as well."

I sat there in amazement. I couldn't believe I was being offered this amazing opportunity. He continued to tell me more about the job.

"Your new boss will be Mark Alexander. He's the Vice President of the company and a great leader. You both are very personable, so you will get along fine with him. When you are a project manager, you won't be restricted to certain subjects anymore, such as social studies or math. With this position, you will get to manage projects in all subject areas. You may have a few different projects going on at the same time, but don't worry, they will more than likely have different deadlines. There's a process that has to be followed for each project, including things like the profit analysis and the actual project plan/schedule. You create the project plan and you will then pass it along to the business analyst who handles that particular subject area. So, as you can see, it all starts with the project manager. You control the schedule and the deadlines. You and all the other project managers will also be required to attend a meeting with Mr. Jamison, Mark and me once a week to keep us updated on the status of your projects."

"Wow Mr. Ford, that's a lot! I sure hope I can handle all of that," I said, scared to death. He noticed I was terrified about this new position. I'm sure he's had to deal with this before.

"Shayla, you will be fine. There are people here to help you. We aren't going to let you fail, trust me" he said with confidence. "Oh, there's one more thing I should tell you. We prefer our project managers already have their Masters degree or a PMP certification or are at least working toward one of those. It would be nice if you get them both. It would make a huge difference in your pay. Just a friendly little hint," he said, raising his eyebrows. I guess that is code for get them both anyway!

"Thanks for your confidence in me, Mr. Ford, I really appreciate it," I said.

"Please call me Sam. Mr. Ford is my father," he said, as we both cracked up laughing. I took a deep breath as I got up.

"Thanks again Mr...I mean, Sam," I said as I shook his hand. "I'm going to go pack up my office now."

"You're quite welcome, and congratulations to you! When you get to the eighth floor, please see Shauna. She's Mark's executive assistant. She will show you where your new office is and also introduce you to your assistant as well."

"My assistant? I'm getting an assistant?" I said shocked.

"Of course you are! You are a manager now, Shayla, so all of those little things you never had time to do, you won't have to worry about it. Your assistant can do it for you."

"Oh my gosh!" I said overwhelmed. "This day just keeps getting better" I said as I left Mr. Ford's office.

I took the elevator back down to the third floor to my office. I was on a natural high. I couldn't believe what just took place. When I got back to my office, Marilyn and the other two business analysts from our group and our former intern Jennifer was there with a cake and a gift.

"Congratulations Shayla!" They all screamed in unison. I was so surprised.

"Aww…. Thanks you all, how did you know?"

"I was the only one that really knew," said Marilyn. Mr. Ford told me yesterday and I got a cake on my way in today."

"Y'all are too much! I really appreciate this," I said.

"Congratulations Shayla" said Janet. I'm so happy for you girl, you deserve it"

"I'm proud of you, young lady," said Jerome. "You da big dog now I see."

"Aww Jerome, you are a mess, thanks!" I said, giving him a hug.

I couldn't handle all of this attention. I am a person who does not like attention of any kind. I was glad the congratulations stuff was almost over.

"Shayla, you stood up to Deborah for me when I was an intern and I really didn't have any more problems out of her after you did and I am forever grateful to you for that. Congratulations to you" said Jennifer, tearing up and giving me a hug.

"Oh girl, you're going to make me cry too!" I said. "Thank you so much for your kind words and well wishes. Not a problem about Deborah. I wasn't going to let her mess with you like that."

"I have a surprise for you," said Jennifer. Guess who your replacement is?"

"Who?" I said cutting my eye.

"Me," said Jennifer, quite bubbly.

"For real? OMG! Congratulations to you," I said hugging her.

"Yeah, she will be in here with me, so now I have another little sister to school," said Marilyn. We all cracked up.

"Okay y'all, lets eat some cake," said Janet. I will cut it."

We all enjoyed the cake and drank some punch as we sat around and talked about my new job. Jennifer offered to stay and help me pack up my office. She is such a sweetheart. I am certainly going to take her up on her offer.

"I'll be right back to help you Shayla. I'm going to go grab some water," said Jennifer.

"Okay, thanks," I said.

The phone rang and it was my good friend Daniel. I could tell something was wrong because I could hear it in his voice. He sounded upset. His ex-wife Candice is one crazy chick. He thought she had moved on with the man she left him for, but apparently things aren't going that well for them because she's too busy trying to make his life hell. He told me some time ago that he had been having trouble with her harassing him about bringing other women around their twins, which is ridiculous, because Daniel is not like that at all. He's only dated one person since the divorce and he's still with her. It took him a long time to get to this point. He finally introduced the kids to Jamie a little while ago and Candice went ballistic when he told her what he was planning to do.

"So let me get this straight. This broad cheats on you and leaves you for her lover and now she's trying to make your life miserable," I said fuming for him.

"Yep, that's what it looks like. She's unbelievable Shayla. You know I would never bring my kids around random women," he said.

"Daniel, I know. You would never do anything that reckless. She's messing with you. Don't let that woman get into your head," I said.

"I'm trying not to, but I just can't believe she's coming at me like that. You're not going to believe what she did this past weekend," he said chuckling a little.

"Oh my, please enlighten me on her latest antics," I said, anxiously awaiting the story.

"Jamie and I went out to dinner Saturday and as we were about to leave the restaurant, someone walked up to the car on Jamie's side and started banging on the window and screaming and cussing. I was like, who the hell is that? Jamie looked terrified. After a couple minutes, I realized it was Candice's crazy ass. She was screaming at Jamie saying 'stay away from my kids you bitch'." Now what I'm trying to figure out is how the hell did she know we were there? She must have followed us or something.

"Wow, you've got to be kidding me right," I said in amazement.

"I wish I was," he said, chuckling some more. "Yo, it was wild! I jumped out of the car to confront her, she was going on, and on about me having women around our kids and she's taking me back to court to modify the visitation order and all this other craziness. I didn't realize the doors were unlocked and I certainly didn't expect what happened next. She opened the door and tried to pull Jamie out of the car. I stopped her before she could hurt her. I told her deranged ass to leave us alone and to get a life. She gets in her car and Jamie and I leave. I'm apologizing repeatedly to Jamie and assuming this episode is over until we get on the beltway to go home. This crazy chick is following us closely down Interstate 495. I tried to speed up and she followed me even closer. Jamie had this "WTF" look on her face and I just couldn't believe this was all happening like this. She chased us for a good five minutes and then I decided to call the police. I described what was happening and gave them her vehicle description and tag number. They were in the process of locating an officer near our location. The stupid police told me to pull over and I said 'ARE YOU CRAZY? THIS WOMAN IS ON MY BUMPER. I'M NOT PULLING OVER!' They finally locate us and make her pull over. They assured me they would take it from there. They gave her a ticket for reckless driving. I felt like that wasn't enough. I think they should have locked her ass up. I was trying to get Jamie to press charges against her for assault, but she didn't want to. Now Jamie is questioning me like something is going on between me and Candice. She's wondering why an ex-wife is acting this obsessive if nothing is going on. I assured her there is absolutely NOTHING going on between Candice and me," he said.

"Daniel, this is like something out of a movie. What the hell is her problem? I can't believe she's acting like that over you and Jamie. She's the one who wanted the divorce and now she can't deal with the decision she's made. Wow, this just blows me," I said, chuckling.

"I'm just glad my kids weren't around to witness this foolishness," he said.

"Yeah, me either" I said.

"Okay Shayla, I gotta get back to work. I have to go to Waldorf for an install. I'll holla at you later," he said.

"Alright Daniel, talk to you later" I said hanging up the phone.

Just as I hung up Jennifer came back in to help me pack up my office. Shauna sent someone down already to pick up my stuff. I gave Marilyn a big hug as I left our office. The wall on my side was so bare now.

"I'm going to miss working in here with you Marilyn. You aren't just a co-worker to me, but an amazing friend as well," I said tearing up a little.

"I'm going to miss you too Shayla, but at least we will still be in the same building, just not in the same office space. We will still be working together because my projects have to be approved by you now," she said with a smile. "Girl, get your behind up to the eighth floor before you make me ruin my makeup and start crying," she said as we both let out a small chuckle.

"See you around girl, and come visit me sometime and I will do the same" I said as I took one last look at our office before walking out the door.

I got on the elevator and that witch, Deborah, was in there trying to pretend not to see me. I couldn't stand her ass and the feeling was mutual. I guess I'm the only one not scared of her.

"Hi Deborah" I said as I rolled my eyes up in my head.

"Shayla" she said still staring forward and looking like she couldn't wait to get off the elevator. The button for the eighth floor was lit so she must have been going to see Mr. Ford or one of the other big wigs up there. The bell chimed, the doors opened, and we both got off heading in the same direction. Shauna was sitting at her desk waiting to greet us.

"Aren't you in the wrong neighborhood Shayla," Deborah said, as she snickered under her breath.

"Excuse me?" I said, as I looked her straight in her eyes while raising my eyebrows.

Shauna had an "oh shit" look on her face.

"Why are you up here on the eighth floor?" she said, looking curious.

"Well Deborah, you must not have gotten the memo. I've been promoted to project manager, so now I work up here on the eighth floor, so you see, I'm in the right neighborhood. I didn't get lost and wander up here like you thought I did. Oh, and for future reference, if I were you, I would stop fuckin' with me because HR is watching you," I said.

Deborah stood there shocked and looking terrified now. She couldn't get away fast enough.

"Umm, Shauna, is Sam in," she said nervously.

"Yes, he's in his office. You can go right in," Shauna said, trying not to laugh.

Deborah power-walked down the hall so fast it wasn't even funny.

"Hi Shayla, I'm Shauna, Mr. Alexander's assistant. Let me show you to your new office.

"Hi Shauna" I said shaking her hand. "It's so nice to meet you, thanks." We walked down the hall in the opposite direction of Sam Ford's office.

"Here we are, this is your office," she said, throwing her hands up.

"Whoa, this is nice, and check out this view" I said in amazement.

"Yeah, it's pretty nice isn't it? You can see the Verizon Center from here," she said. "I'll let you go ahead and get settled. If you need anything, just press 3 to call me or press 5 for your assistant Kera. She's running around here somewhere, but when she gets back, I'm sure she will come in and introduce herself to you," she said as she left my office.

The eighth floor was the bomb! There were some nice cubicles in the office area outside of my office that I assume belonged to the assistants. My office was very nice and a little bigger than my last office. I'm sure it's going to feel weird having an office to myself. There was a beautiful cherry wood desk with a leather chair behind it. I sat in it to get a feel for it and it was very comfortable. They had already moved my computer upstairs as well so that was convenient. There was also a leather sofa on the other side of my office as well as a little round table with a couple chairs around it. There was a beautiful fruit basket on the table that I hadn't noticed when I first walked in. I guess I was so in awe over the office. I walked over to the table and admired the fruit basket. It looked delicious! It also had a bottle of my favorite sparkling cider in it as well. There was an envelope attached to it with my name on it. I opened it and it was a nice welcome card. It read: SHAYLA, WELCOME TO THE TEAM! WE ARE GLAD YOU ARE HERE. VERY RESPECTFULLY, MARK ALEXANDER.

"Oh wow, that is so nice," I said aloud, as I read the card.

"I thought so, too," said this nice smooth voice behind me. "Hi, I'm Mark Alexander, you must be Shayla, welcome!" he said shaking my hand. I was stunned because Mr. Alexander was fine as hell. He stood about six-foot-one, had an athletic build, probably around two hundred five pounds. He wore a nice dark blue suit, had a close haircut and a stunning smile.

"Yes, yes I am, thanks so much for this wonderful basket, Mr. Alexander. It's nice to finally meet you. That was very nice of you," I said nervously.

"Likewise. Please call me Mark and you're very welcome, Shayla. Do you go by Shayla, or would you like to be called something else?" he asked.

"No," I said shaking my head. "Shayla is fine."

"Well how do you like your new office?" he asked, looking around as if he had never been in here before.

"I love it, it's beautiful," I said.

"I'm glad you approve. Well, I see you haven't quite settled in yet, so I'll let you do that. Let me know if you need anything. I gotta run. My brother is supposed to be coming by to get me for lunch. See you later," he said as he left my office.

"See you later," I said.

I looked around my office and saw that I needed to start unpacking these boxes and putting my other things on the wall. As I unpacked one of the boxes, there was a knock on my door.

"Hi Shayla, I'm Kera, your assistant, it's good to meet you," she said walking into my office and shaking my hand.

Kera was a very professional young lady. Looked to be about my sisters age with a fierce short hair cut similar to the one Toni Braxton use to wear when her first album came out. She was medium brown, around five-foot-one and maybe one hundred ten pounds. I was impressed with how she was dressed. She wore a tan business dress with boots and she had on this beautiful scarf as well.

"Hi Kera, it's very nice to meet you," I said, getting up off the floor and brushing myself off.

"Are you finding everything you need?" she said.

"Well, I've just been unpacking and trying to get settled in so far. I can't really think of anything I may need yet." I sat down on the couch.

"Well, when you get a second, make me a list and I'll get everything you need for your office, and if there's anything in here you don't like, even the couch, I can have it replaced for you."

"Wow, really? The furniture is great, everything's great so far. Thanks."

"I know you are getting settled in, but may I have five minutes of your time to go over your schedule for this afternoon?"

She opened the organizer on her lap that read: **SHAYLA RICHARDSON** on the front.

"Um, my schedule?" I said, surprised.

"Yes, ma'am. I am the assistant to three project managers— you, Ronda and James—so I like to take about ten to fifteen minutes with each of you in the morning to go over your schedule. I'm just now getting to you because I know you've been trying to settle in this afternoon, so I didn't want to bother you."

I was impressed with this young lady's organizational skills. She explained why my name was on the front because it was my schedule. She probably had one for each of us. We went over the schedule pretty quickly and I got back to unpacking.

"Welcome again, and let me know if you need anything," she said as she left my office.

"Thank you, Kera, I appreciate it!"

As I was unpacking one of the boxes, I heard Mr. Alexander talking to someone as he walked down the hall. His voice was getting closer and closer and he was about to walk past my office until I heard him say, "Oh, Price, let me introduce you to one of my new project managers." He knocked on my office door.

"Hey, Shayla, I want you to meet my brother. Price this is Shayla."

"Hello, Shayla" he said in his masculine voice. "It's good to meet you. My brother here says you are very sharp."

I looked up at him with a modest smile. "It's nice to meet you, Price, and thanks for the compliment."

Price Alexander was very attractive. A little taller and slimmer than his brother though. I'm guessing he was around six-feet-three inches tall. Good looks definitely ran in the family.

"Would you like to join us for lunch? Bro, you don't mind do you?" he said as he faced Mark.

"No, not at all," Mark said, shaking his head.

"I really wish I could, but I've been trying to get unpacked all afternoon."

"Oh, that's too bad. Well, maybe another time then?" he said, looking straight at me. I didn't know what to say at first. I froze a little. Mark was observing his little brother, getting his mack on.

"Sure that would be fine," I said. His eyes were still on me.

"Okay, we better get going then, I have to get back here by two o'clock for a meeting," said Mark.

"Enjoy your lunch guys," I said.

"It was really nice meeting you Shayla," said Price.

"You, too," I said.

Like I said earlier, could this day get any better? The answer to that question was yes because it just had! He continued to look at me as he left my office....

Bianca's Thoughts:

Wow!! Things are really starting to look up for Shayla! You go girl!

Unexpected Interest

Not aware that I was being noticed,
A gentle person had arrived
He entered into my view unexpectedly,
Our eyes locked by surprise

Not realizing I was about to make a new friend,
The unexpected interest I would surely see again
I was oblivious to what was going on, But soon I realized
    chemistry was born

Not expecting anything on that day,
Little by little we began to play
Laughter filled the church,
The unexpected interest was gentle and kind

Not realizing I would hug him the next day,
A voice inside said, "Don't let him walk away."
I hugged him for a second time,
His skin now very close to mine

Not realizing that this was my time, to explore yet another friend
The unexpected interest has appeared in my life again

Epilogue

UPDATES

Interesting how things have been happening for Shayla and most of her friends.

Kathy is still the same outspoken person she's always been. She keeps in touch with Shayla and they make a real effort to get out sometimes.

Monique is still at it. She has been carrying on an affair with the same guy for almost a year now. I'm sure her husband, Calvin, is not that stupid and knows what's going on. He's so in love with her that he's probably just going to accept what's going on and continue to put up with her infidelity. I truly feel sorry for people like him who feel like they have to stay in situations like that and have taken on the attitude they can't do better. That sounds like a self-esteem issue to me. If you know someone is continuously being unfaithful to you and you chose to stay, then there's something terribly wrong with your self-esteem. Why put up with someone who comes home when they feel like it, or sometimes not at all?

Melanie is on the road to recovery. Her depression problem is getting better and she has been seeing her psychologist again to help her through her problems. It has done her a world of good. The kids are doing great and she still maintains a nice co-parent relationship with their dad.

Daniel is doing well. He and his new girlfriend, Jamie, are about to celebrate a year together. His ex-wife, Candice, is still up to her usual antics, which sometimes causes stress in his relationship.

Ashley is in her last year of law school and has been focused on finishing. She is still the same spoiled brat she's always been, but Shayla loves her little sister dearly. Ashley has learned a few lessons about men and dating over the last few years herself.

Allen and Tracey are legally separated and are in the process of getting a divorce. Allen was willing to make the marriage work, but Tracey was determined to get out. Thankfully, little Kennedy was too young to know what was going on between her parents.

Marilyn is still giving out great advice. I don't think she realizes how much of a blessing she is to those in her life. She has helped Shayla through some very tough situations.

Shayla has learned a lot these past couple of years. She is doing very well in her new position. As for her experiences with love, she is not going to harp on the bad experiences. She is just going to look at each one as a learning experience. Her father gave her this quote one day and it makes perfect sense: "When things don't work out in life, don't keep playing it in your head over and over and stressing over what you would have done differently. Just move on and learn from the experience." She's going to take that advice to heart as she is about to embark on this new chapter in her life. She is not going to give up on love. Can Price possibly be her Mr. Right? Stay tuned...

www.ingramcontent.com/pod-product-compliance
Lightning Source LLC
Chambersburg PA
CBHW071350170626
46811CB00003B/1068

were constantly scrutinized, whether they were in a Store or not. *A King must always display elegance, grace, and compassion...* one of the tenants read. Another Customer always had to give up their seat to a King if asked, no matter where, and other Customers were required to 'pay tribute' when demanded, no matter what.

Far removed from the Kitchen, King's were free moving agents within a Store. Any aisle, Kitchen, or Bistro at any time could be paid a visit. Thus every inch of every Store had to be refreshed and well kept daily.

Another key item separating King's from the rest was access to information. The principal example of this is the exact number and location of all Customers worldwide. This information was kept privy for those at this level out of security and the interest of self-preservation. The idea was that by keeping the number of King's limited, and crucial information on ranks privileged, the cause could survive regardless of any attack from the UN. Cut one head off...

This was all well and good for Clancy for about a decade. But after several meetings turned down the path of the routine, a moribund feeling set in.

Clancy took to the Annals; a vast information trove on the history and lore of Customer Buttcheeks maintained in the Flagship Store in London. His research had yielded the potential existence of an even higher rank. The raw data was scant, but the premise, the very foundation of another rank, was sound.

"'Complete a task of Epic/
Climb the Mountain and own it..."'

Clancy would often repeat the words he discovered by rote. After finding the word 'Imperator' near the same cluster of information, Clancy himself dubbed the rank 'Customer Imperator', or Emperor Customer.

As a King, Clancy had been invited to wear noise-cancelling headphones during an Executive Session of the Extraordinary Council of World Governance in New Thebes while it was docked in Port Moresby. His belief was such that were he to reach the rank of Customer Imperator, he would be able to remove the headphones and participate in world building. Once on the inside, he believed, perhaps, he could undo several things that he felt were less than advantageous for the populous being governed.

Clancy had aimed high, and this unprecedented, undefeated season was his way to hit the target with gusto.

Niko shuffled into the changing room complex to divest from his duties. Upon reaching his locker, Niko immediately noticed a glimmering sliver of paper peeking out from his locker. He began his routine and slyly tucked the note into the elastic band of his boxer-briefs.

He took his time getting ready. The others quickly donned their street clothes and filed towards the tunnel leading to the gallery of Rosenbridge doorways. When Niko knew he was the last one in the locker room, he unfolded the note and began reading:

Nikolaus, are you for real,
or are you just playing the game?
—MD

Niko read the short note several times. He could smell sandal wood esters rising up from the shiny paper. The expansive scent brought back an image of Margeaux Drexler, her thin upper lip, her flattering overbite, and that luxuriant hair.

Reasoning this note had to be from Margeaux, he chose to be "for real", although how soon he would be able to tell her he was not sure. Truthfully,

Niko had no idea when or if he would be transferred back here to the London Store.

He got up and trotted after the others, not wanting to hang back too long and raise suspicion. Niko scanned the faces he could make out in the low light and din of the Victorian-decorated waiting area. The soft carpet and intricate tapestry curtains that draped over large windows looking out onto a traditional English garden made for delicious eye candy. The room smelled lightly of vanilla and dry tobacco. At the far end, a bellhop stood at a shimmering brass set of controls and rotated wall after wall of doors in and out of their moorings to his right. Three doors at a time would appear along with each wall; the separate doors leading to separate locales.

Just as Niko resigned himself to running into Margeaux at some point in the distant future, her scent wafted by his nose. He frantically looked around and at last noticed her in the on-deck area of the elaborate exit system.

"Margeaux!" He called out to the back of her head.

She abruptly turned and made eye contact.

Niko rehashed the public shaming by Clancy, the look from Margeaux in the aftermath, and the things he had been reading about the organization on the ultranet and called out "I'm for real!"

Some of the others present looked up and wondered what the Clerk III was doing. Most just shuffled forward in his or her line as it shrunk with each departing member. Margeaux smiled, gave him a wink, and hopped through her door when it was made ready.

Later that night, Niko stood on his balcony, his small tablet in his left hand, a watering can in his right. The frangipani specimens his botanist cousin in LA had sent him were flourishing, as were the various species of mushrooms, cannabis, and pitcher plants he meticulously maintained.

Niko finished watering his delicates and scaled the bamboo scaffolding he had erected that lead to the roof of his building. Up here, several tenants had setup greenhouses or other similar facilities and systems for plants that may emit odors or excessive pollen, etc.

The path that began at the top of his scaffolding eventually wound its way to his pride and joy. This path had been lined with carefully plotted bamboo and orchids of various species and maturity. The orchids had been carefully placed in hanging, ad-hoc misshapen glass planters. These seemingly random chunks of melted sand Niko had collected as cast-offs from a local crucible. Their varying colors and rhomboidal polygonal forms were easy on the eyes, given the way Niko had sewn them into the living tapestry that led to his most cherished botanical possession: a massive Rafflesia.

Niko's Rafflesia, dubbed 貴乃花(Takanohana), rested comfortably in its own large glass bowl with a hard-carved gold lettered name plate. Sympathetic plants grew in the soil beneath it and thrived. The thick and ropey tendrils of the flower draped down Niko's bamboo construct and formed an overhang on top of his balcony; the plant grew as if it knew exactly where Niko lived.

From this roof top greenery, Niko could see his place of employment. LeRoy's Narcofloria #427 was all lit up. The night crowd was always a bit rougher than the day-trippers, but the overall experience was still great when compared to where he could be working. Beyond this outcropping of UN-managed modernization were the rolling hills of tea terraces the region was famous for. Niko could see members of the Indo-Scotch-Viet commune that tended the crops completing their end-of-day tasks, wrapped in the tartan cloth their of respective clans. All devotees dyed their hair red and also tended to vast herds of sheep, bees, hemp, and of course, the teaworks themselves. The night was warm and Niko reacted to a long font of sweat that trickled down from his neck to his chest. He adjusted the watering system that fed Takanohana and stroked a few of the large, imposing vermillion petals.

As Niko turned and began the descent to his balcony, a behelmed carrier pigeon arrived. The small bird landed on Niko's shoulder and extended its right foot, displaying a shiny gold scroll tube.

He plucked the dainty delivery from the pigeon

and held out his ID scramble. A blue laser emitted from the center of the golden helmet the avian courier was wearing and it scanned the unique identifier. An approving squawk was issued, and the iridescent blue bird departed.

The scroll read as follows:

I could be Decommissioned for how I got your info, but I feel that is inevitable. If you really are for real, meet me at The Golden Petal in Little Tibet, 1600 tomorrow. -MD

Niko ran his thumb over the raised letters on the small scroll. The glossy ink hummed as the ridges of his fingerprints glided over. With Sachin still working his shift at TASC, Niko connected his VPN and entered the last few onionlinks he could remember.

Not long after, he was in.

Mysterious   group   behind   recent terror?

Who, or what, is a 'Customer'?

...My father joined some group, he would never say the name, but not long after joining, he was dead...

Never, at all ever, call the number

161

in those weird infomercials...

Niko, like most of his age group, had read these and various other tales from the 'net. Opinions varied greatly; some believed and others believed in portions. Most believed there was *some* truth to at least part of it, but with their relative positions in the world being so cushy and flooded with ease, they chose to not investigate further.

Niko pressed on through the sob stories and horror-drenched yarns until he found a sheet of phrases. The OP* held that these seven phrases could open doors held shut within the organization.

For example, if one is ever in an unsavory situation with another Customer, simply state "I'd like to speak with your manager." This granted an audience with the offending member's superior, something the offender may want to steer clear of.

There was also "But it's on sale." This verbal key allowed one to take something home from a Store; an item on a shelf, a to-go box, another Customer...

Another one that stood out, due to its blistering obviousness, was "The customer is always right." This provided one with escape from any given situation involving other Customers. If someone, anyone, questions what you're doing or saying, simply drop the line and you're left alone. Although he was already aware of this phrase, he had been in the dark as to its additional power.

What does it all mean? Niko pondered over his findings and how they could relate to his particular station. Margeaux, despite ranking very high, was

Original Poster

clearly put-off by Clancy's chastisement of her father. He wondered how long she had been Shopping and why she had opened up to him.

Niko scrolled through a few more pages, until he came across an account purporting to ID Customer Buttcheeks as the culprit in the training facility fire at the London PolyMatic Football Palace. He pored over the details and screenshots. After twenty minutes of examination and cross-referencing the sources, Niko reasoned that Customer Buttcheeks had indeed participated in some capacity in the fracas. For him, it was the shipping records that did it. In the middle of several walls-of-text was a picture of a delivery manifesto. Oliver Monkton, a mid-level trainer and fully-ensconced Customer, signed for the delivery of a new Amplified Botanical Healing Apparatus (or, ABHA). The large coffin-like device was wheeled in and parked outside the home weight room.

A still from a security camera revealed a spark of some nature emitting from the ABHA. Said spark then grew into a blaze. The tall flames fed on an oxygen leak in the side of the just-so-happened-to-be-damaged-in-transit-ABHA. The blaze killed several people and crippled the London Gentry's ability to train in the off-season.

After reliving the tragedy, Niko remembered the bitter feelings Clancy maintained towards Saxby Lawless and the entire Amplified Gentry organization. With each passing second, Niko suddenly began to see a correlation between Customer Buttcheeks and several terrorist-like activities around the world.

At the onset, Niko just wanted to be a part of something, and his innate curiosity is brought him into his first Store in the beginning. Most people deny this organization even exists, and yet here he is, rapidly rising through the ranks.

I didn't want to be a part of something like this… Niko thought, sinking into his chair.

Shortly thereafter, Niko surmised there was no easy way out of the organization. He set an alarm for 1600 to meet Margeaux.

At 1550, Niko sat down in a booth at The Golden Petal, a secluded and private local tea and ramen house. The ebullient server stopped by and took his order: a small bowl of baingan bhurta, some naan, a small bowl of tonokotsu ramen with black garlic oil and three ajitsuke eggs, all together with creamy iced Bai Miang tea. The woman smiled and left, her yellow sari twinkling with trinkets and charms.

Margeaux arrived at 1600 on the dot and sat herself across from Niko.

"Have you ordered?" Margeaux skipped a 'hello' and got down to business.

"Y-yea, I ordered-"

"I don't care, I'll eat from whatever you got," she placed her bag inside the booth and got settled. "So, you say you're for real," Margeaux eyed him with the intensity of a coronal mass ejection. "Why?"

The waitress swung by with Niko's tea and he signaled that Margeaux would be having the same.

"Well, I read some accounts on the UltraNet and-"

"Whose?"

For a time, Niko said nothing. He was a little intimidated by the woman's severity, but also enchanted. He worked to get his thoughts in order so as to not further make a fool of himself and waste any more of her time.

"The users were anon's."

"Hmm. You know there are fake's, right? CB puts out false accounts to keep the mythos strong. What *exactly* did you read?"

"The one that stands out the most for me is the fire in London."

"How did it start?"

"A CB worker accepted a damaged ABHA, and-"

"Good, I wrote that," she cut in. "So, you really are for real," she said while analyzing him with an ever increasing intensity. "Good. Good..."

The waitress brought Margeaux her tea, and she took a long sip of the creamy and smoky emulsion.

"How long have you been *Ensconced?*" She asked without blinking.

"Nine months," Niko said mechanically.

"Really? That's it? And you're already a Clerk III?"

"I guess... Clancy likes me?"

"Hmm… indeed."

The waitress arrived with Niko's food along with a second set of flatware for Margeaux.

"Is your place nearby?" Margeaux asked.

"Yea, it's a few blocks west."

"Ok, we'll eat here and finish talking there."

Margeaux tore a piece of naan and covered it in the bhurta. Niko worked to get in several long ocular assessments of her beauty. He kept his admiration clandestine for now, as he had no idea where this was headed. She could be a spy, set to root out insurgency. She could also be genuinely looking for a way out and perhaps doesn't have time for love at the moment.

After the meal, the pair walked to Niko's flat. Sachin was out with his girlfriend Fatima, so Niko knew that he had a few hours and didn't need to rush.

The seventh flight of stairs was usually where people began to gripe, but Margeaux plodded up the steps in her green heels without protest.

Niko unlocked the door and allowed Margeaux to enter first.

"Sorry it's a wreck, we are two men after all…" Niko was more so apologizing for Sachin's unkemptness. Niko's portion of the flat was organized and relatively tidy. Margeaux remained silent as she looked around the room.

Suddenly, Margeaux waved her hands frantically, trying to get Niko's attention.

"What is it?" he asked.

She quickly raised a finger to her lips, indicating a call for silence. Niko complied and waited for what was next.

Margeaux moved some stacked papers out of the way and revealed a silver insect-like device. She showed Niko the recording apparatus and returned the 'creature' to its locus.

With one perfectly structured finger she pointed up, indicating the roof. Niko astutely nodded and led her to his balcony-garden and from there to the ladder.

Margeaux let out a breath of astonishment at the initial sight of Niko's garden. Fireflies were engaging in a waltz amongst the bamboo grove. In a small and deliberate hollow Margeaux could see bioluminescent mushrooms slowly progressing through an intense range of colors. The pair eventually settled on a wooden bench near a mossy outcropping beside Takanohana and at last she spoke.

"I knew something wasn't right. No one climbs that fast. Who are you, really?" Margeaux seemed convinced that Niko was some sort of key player.

"I-I'm Nikolaus... that's who I am," his bottom lip began to quiver ever so slightly.

"Ok..." Margeaux tucked her lips in and slowly knitted her brow. With a swift and sudden jerk, she thrust out her hand and pricked his left fingertip with a pin. The resultant blood she quickly collected and placed several drops of into a small golden lily she had produced.

"Ouch! What the-"

"Quiet!" she sharply charged.

The lily spun and then emitted a precision ding.

She brought out her handheld device to interpret the results.

"Hmm, Nikolaus... so you're not lying..." Margeaux returned her equipment to their respective pockets and she resumed her death stare. "Have you preformed any *sexual* favors?"

"Ok, I don't know who *you* really are, and frankly I'm uncomfortable going any further with this." Niko was miffed by the whole experience and now worried his own life may be in danger.

Margeaux laughed endearingly and slid closer to Niko.

"Look," she started then stopped. She took her time and drew a breath of the hot and sweet night air. "I'm sorry. But I have to be careful. I've reached out before to others and... let's just say it hasn't worked out too well. After our conversation in London, I left feeling like you were different; not like the average Customer," Margeaux shifted her stance and put her bag down.

"When you said you wrote that account," Niko started.

"I did. I wrote it because it's true. *I* hacked the security cams. *I* took the screenshots. *I* uploaded the moving images of maimed body parts. All of it. To put it plainly, Clancy needs to be stopped."

"Clancy?"

"Yes. He's running the show, and he has no idea about the Truth."

"'The Truth'?"

Margeaux laughed again, this time with an appreciative

air.

"You really aren't like the rest of them; thank God!" She nearly shouted. "I was starting to genuinely lose hope! How did you access my post?"

"Here I'll- wait, we can't go inside, huh?"

"I'd prefer not to be recorded and killed, so…"

"Gotcha, I setup a VPN the last time I traveled to Edo. I just connect to that and bore through the darknet until I find something worthwhile."

"Look, I don't want to sound pushy or desperate, but… If I'm being honest, I'm alone in my thinking and feeling. Everyone else is committed. To the death. But, I believe you when you say you aren't."

"At this point, after what I've read and what we saw Clancy do… I think I made a mistake in rapping at that green door across from LeRoy's, when it was there."

Margeaux studied Niko in silence for several more seconds.

"Do you have a girlfriend?" She asked plainly.

Niko's heart sunk. *Did she really just ask that?*

In his mind, Niko imagined a man driving up to him in a rickshaw who, upon hopping out, hands him a briefcase with several billion gold-dollars in it. *How could all of that possibly fit into one briefcase?*

Now in a sweat, Niko stammered in a wobbly voice, "N-no, not at the moment…"

"Good," Margeaux said, shortly before moving in to kiss him on the mouth. "If we're really going to do this, we need to be fully honest and open with each other. If you cross me, I *will* kill you. Otherwise… I am yours, and you are mine."

The schoolyard-sounding events swirled in Niko's mind. This goddess had claimed him and his loyalty with nothing more than an abundance of cunning intelligence and good looks. With the direction the things in the organization and in his life had been going as of late, Niko was really just up for anything unusual. The fact that she was educated, gorgeous, and angry were all bonuses; a delightful banchan to the already delicious beebimbop.

"So now that we're *Associated*, we need to work at the same branch. Do you want me to come here?"

"You know, I've always been fascinated with London," Niko intoned.

"Really?" Margeaux said with a blush. "Do you want to come to my store?"

"Y-Yeah, Sachin can deal, he's starting to get on my nerves. But there is one thing…"

"What's that?"

"I *will not* cheer for the Gents…"

Margeaux leaned in and Niko could feel her breath on his ear. *"Then, Let's Go Death…"* she tenderly whispered into his ear, before pulling back.

"Unfortunately *I* must go now," she said.

"Ok," he was taken by her abruptness. "When and how do we get in touch?"

"I'll take care of the paperwork for your transfer, and until then I'll keep sending pigeons, I won't trust the airwaves or mail channels."

"I-I'll think of you."

"I'll make it easy then," Margeaux said. She

smoothly removed a jewel encrusted alloy bobby pin from her river of hair and slipped it onto the collar of his shirt.

Niko lead Margeaux down the stairs and out onto the street. The couple kissed and he flagged down a rickshaw.

"When's your next meeting?" Margeaux asked, her eyes glittered in the reflected light.

"On Wednesday, at 1900."

It was Monday.

"Your transfer will be ready by then, bye," Margeaux said while scrunching up her face and crossing her eyes in a radiant, modern, display of beauty.

Niko watched the rickshaw disappear around a corner and then shot back upstairs. The wave of endorphins engulfing his mind was almost overwhelming. *Had it been real? Does she really want me, or to just bring down the organization? Seeing your step-father publicly humiliated like that though... All those random pills...*

After a couple of hours of Southern-fried sludge metal and cannabis, Sachin walked in the door.

"'Sup." The dark skinned Sikkimese regarded Niko with something close to suspicion. Niko kept his wits about him and proceeded as normal.

"Hey, how was your shift?"

"Typical," Sachin moved carefully through the small apartment and made his way to the fridge. He groped around, not really looking for anything in particular. After several seconds, he withdrew a bottle full of clear liquid from the rear of the cold box. He unscrewed the cap and took several burning gulps. He wiped his mouth and fixed his gaze on the back of Niko's head.

"How long, Niko? Eh?" Sachin's voice had an emptiness Niko had never heard before.

Right away, Niko knew what Sachin meant.

"How long what, Satch?"

Several more searing gulps of white lightning.

"How long before you stopped lying to me?"

"I'm sorry?"

"Yes, you are," Sachin's pulse was picking up. "You've been going there at least once a week for…"

"Nine months," Niko dropped the coy act.

"…Nine months," Sachin repeated with a terse hollowness. "I can't believe I've been living so close to you…"

Niko was surprised by Sachin's demeanor. Up to this point, the two hadn't really been brothers per say, but they were close friends. As he engaged the situation, he looked back in his mind and realized he had no idea of Sachin's past.

"My mother… *they* killed my mother… *You* belong to '*they*'… Get out." Sachin disseminated the findings of his rudimentary investigation into his mother's death.

Niko's jaw dropped.

"Now. Pack your things and leave the whole of India. If you don't… I will have no choice but to *hunt* you," Sachin was wide-eyed and unblinking.

"Satch, I don't know what to-"

"Leave!" Although Sachin revealed a rusty blade, he would not reveal, though, how he learned of Niko's membership.

"Ok! Ok!" Niko put his hands up and went to retrieve the bag he had already packed, following word from Margeaux. Niko gathered what other things he could, and glanced at the balcony.

My plants…

"Out!"

"Satch, I'm *going* to say goodbye to Takanohana," Niko was resolute.

Sachin stepped aside and let Niko out onto the balcony. The large flower greeted Niko with slight undulations.

"Takanohana, the great Yokozuna," Niko said while caressing the imposing crimson petals. "I've been kicked out big guy. But I will be back. I will return for you and the others, and we'll pick up right where we left off."

Takanohana shuddered violently.

Niko had never seen this, or any plant, shudder. His careful observation during the tremor led him to notice a tendril emitting from a crack in the bottom the large planter Takanohana lived in. This vine began in a fissure in the pot and plunged into a fault in the roof. The girth appeared to be around 25 centimeters; substantial even for Takanohana.

"Sorry big guy, but 商売終わり (Shōbai owari). I will be back for you."

The heaving rafflesia shuddered once more and then returned to what Niko perceived to be more

173

pleasant undulations of a satisfactory ilk.

Niko gave the plant one last look before he finished his descent onto the balcony. Turning his attention inside, Niko immediately noticed a light purple miasma that was not present prior to his ascent. Sachin was nowhere in sight. Niko slid the glass door open and was hit by the powerful odor of rotten flesh. He put his hand over his nose and forcefully breathed through his mouth.

As he stepped in, his foot tripped on something that was not there previously.

Niko looked down to see what impeded his ingress. He had tripped on Sachin's left leg. He rotated his head and noticed Sachin's bloated, swollen throat and face. In addition to the swelling, a pox creating pea-sized yellow pustules had also overtaken Sachin's face. Niko then noticed the rusty blade, earlier used to threaten, was now lodged snuggly into Sachin's left lung, as if he fell onto it.

In total disbelief, Niko's eyes darted around the room, scouring the flat for any sign of foul play. Just then, something caught his eye. In the Southeast corner of the room, near the ceiling, a pod of some kind had burst through the stucco. The bloom was beautiful: a thousand violently red petals overflowing from a deep green casing with yellow fractalized, romanesco-like growths jutting out like icebergs. A small purple cloud fizzed and popped as it hung around the exploded bud.

Niko was a stumbling mess as he gathered everything he forgot in a panic. While going for his knapsack, he tripped over Sachin's bloating, cracking, corpse. He swallowed what rose into his mouth and all at once realized there were very few things that he cared about in this space. Niko reasoned that all he really needed for the next step in his life was some clean underwear, his laptop, and his signed Creeping Death jersey.

Where could he go? Niko had no idea. His transfer wouldn't be *Proper and Official* until Wednesday. Without question his initial thought was that of contacting Margeaux. But if she didn't trust the airwaves and the mail-ways, there's no way he was going to hop in bed with them, regardless of the situation.

He put on his best casual facial expression and trotted out of his building with a pinkish and moribund spring in his step.

He turned right and passed by the shops he spent most of his previous life ignoring. There was a candy shop featuring insect-infused sweets from across the whole of the Sub-Continent. Next to that was a Laundromat owned by a quasi-legal order of

African monks. Continuing onward, Niko glided by the other businesses that separated him from his imposing sojourn: a tailor specializing in Amplified spider silk, a Video Cassette emporium, the crematorium that subconsciously caused all in the neighborhood to order take-away barbeque several times a week, and of course the dozens of cafes and flophouse-style narcotic chains.

After a couple of hours, Niko was tired. He turned into the enormous and walled Mansour Mandeep park and gardens. Despite being the middle of the night, there was a sizable number of people milling about. The lights made no sound, as per usual. Niko caught a whiff of cinnamon and night-blooming jasmine.

A memory from his early twenties stepped out of a tuk-tuk and blew smoke in his face.

Once, whilst on a whim-of-a-trip to the Union of Venice, Niko wound up without a place to sleep. A large cruse ship had docked and every lodging spot was swollen with business. He walked from hotel to hotel offering upwards of GD$500 to the various hoteliers for a spot to sleep, even if it were on the floor.

They spat at him. Some cursed him in Amhar'Italian. Either way, they didn't care how much money he had. Their dignity of service simply mattered more.

Niko eventually gave up and sat himself down on a set of cold stairs that led to a bridge out of the floating nation. For a couple of hours, late-night revelers walked by, occasionally chucking a coin or two in his direction.

Time slid by in a fetching gondola. In-between collecting the coins thrown at him and roiling in vagrancy, Niko noticed a walled and gated park. When there was a gap in metallic disk hurlers, he ambled close to the gate and chucked his belongings over the spiked barrier. Another couple passed by, too enamored to even pretend to look for money to throw his way. After an unusually hyperactive child scrambled past, his parents in tow, Niko was up and over the locked wrought iron impedance in a flash.

The small triangular park was quiet. Beyond the entryway was a fountain and several marble benches. He checked the time: 0245am. He set his watch for 0700 and cobbled a sleeping area out of his bags on top of a hidden bench.

He survived the night with only seven mosquito bites.

Itching and undaunted, Niko gathered his things along with himself and walked headfirst into the day…

His stomach was a gravel-filled wine skin.

Watching Sachin, his friend, turn so quickly against him created a gnawing feeling in his chest that hurt more than any hunger could. Niko tried to reason on why the pain of betrayal wouldn't leave.

177

I mean, our meeting was so sudden and random... I took him in after he was kicked out for a violation of a bizarre familial taboo. He goaded me into moving from my rent-controlled two-bedroom into that rat hole with a garden on the roof. Had he ever been my friend? Was he just using me? We were never that close... In fact he rebuffed my camaraderie more often than not.

Niko took the memories of his time with Sachin Tiwary and decided they were of no advantage. The terse experience had certainly changed him for the better, only added to his personality. Niko had learned to jettison regret and to not waste time resenting the less than exemplary people in his life. The people who brought agitation and strife into his existence also brought character and endurance. Hating them and their time in his life was a waste of energy. In the end, they simply weren't worth it.

Niko stole into an Elizabeth-II-style pub and ordered a full English breakfast. He kept his eyes down and spoke to no one but the waiter. He eagerly shoveled the beans, grilled mushrooms, bacon, fried slices, sausages, coddled eggs, and smoked locusts into his mouth. The buttered coffee and mango juice honed his mind and made it ready for the thirty-six hours that stood between the now and his transfer to London.

Niko paid his check and shoved off on foot. The sun was warm and the plants were engorged. Darjeeling was in full bloom, and Niko had just rounded the corner to face the State Bank of India, which was of course now on the UN Interplanetary

Gold Standard. The bank building seemed to hum like a centrifuge. Niko was often repelled by the gold keys he had to carry as a means of currency; the jangling metal chits of various denominations seemed to emit a miasma that no one else was bothered by. As a result of this alleged field of influence, Niko never went into the bank proper. He got his keys from the machine adjacent to the temple-like facility. From across the street he looked at the black marble pillars with gold skirting and the men and women in their designated swallow-tail Capitalist garb climbing and descending the grand staircase. His own key ring was getting light, so he forced himself over to the machine staffed by an Amplified macaque. He wore a tidy green uniform with sparkling brass buttons and a neat pillbox hat.

"Accown numbah, pleese."

"7T9-737 P499," Niko warbled.

The little macaque clacked away on the custom keyboard in front of him. A dark woman in a flattering sari made eye contact with smartly dressed teller and spit into the gutter.

"Thank, how much yoo nid?"

"GD$500."

"Oh, big spendah…"

The macaque initiated the insta-cast and stared blankly at the proprietary UN standardized molten gold alloy while it oozed into the hot machine's intake funnel. Thirty seconds later, the blank keys were cool and in the deft creature's hands.

"May I please have three hundreds, eight twenties, and the rest in singles, thank you."

The macaque made a slight, non-committal, response and went to cut the golden keys to Niko's specifications. The dust that resulted from the cutting fell into a special melting tray that funneled the shavings right back into the bank.

"Here you go, sree hundreds, eight tventies, forty zinglez. Nice day." The creature's voice was a foggy low frequency drone.

The key ring was heavy, but Niko had worked hard to earn every gram of weight thereon.

Niko departed from the bank and its throbbing bamboo forest.

Darjeeling was hot, and it was only 1000am.

At 1100am, Niko found himself on the bank of the River Rangeet. A clutch of River People huddled under a concrete pier roasting something over a fire. With the weather being so warm, Niko puzzled over their closeness to the fire. He turned his attention from their colorful flames and looked over the various boats shooting up and down the enlarged waterway. The river's expansion was mandated not long after the war ended and India emerged as the pace-setting Super Power. New Thebes spent a considerable amount of time docked in Kolkata, and it was during that time many changes were ordered and readily delivered. One of those changes was a vast expansion into the northeast, with a focus on Amplifying the environment. The mighty Rangeet was dredged and converted into a thriving watercourse. However, the locals insisted on the preservation of several natural landscape features, leading to the existence of muddy shore spots, similar to the one Niko found himself in.

The water lapped at the shoreline and invited Niko in. He flexed his toes in his shoes and decided he did not want to risk losing the entirety of his belongings to the quivering mass of River People.

Just as he-

"Psst, hey you."

Niko ignored the call for his attention.

"Hey, psst, you, are you a *Communist?*"

Niko turned his head and looked into the dense foliage, searching for the owner of the voice.

"You, with the *hair… are you a Communist?*"

"No, no I'm not…" Niko said into the thicket of trees and shrubbery.

"Hm, but you *look* like one," the voice continued. "You sure you've never been to *Miami?*"

"Not even on a layover."

The voice chewed over Niko's response.

"I've seen you before…"

"Really," Niko said flatly, facing the river, trying to ignore the voice.

"Yes. I have. If it wasn't in Red Miami, then you must be *Ensconced.*"

That caught Niko's attention.

"Come again?"

"I must've seen you *Shopping* somewhere…"

"Is that so? Y'know, if you have seen me *Shopping*, it's only fair that you ID yourself. I mean, *The Customer-*"

"*Is always right.* Over here."

The operator of the voice revealed itself to be a

rhinoceros with a prominent opaque pink crystalline horn with a sleek black cobra coiled around it. Emerging from the greenery, the dual-beast cautiously entered the visible spectrum of Niko.

"Okie dokie…" Niko was incredulous.

"We are Hammer and Sickle, a creation of Mr. Lake."

Mr. Lake? Niko thought.

"Why did you first ask if I was a Communist if you've seen me *Shopping*?"

"It was an honest question. We thought we'd encountered you at home in the past. We've never been dispatched to India, due to it's sharing a border with Free China."

"Ok, so, why are you here, talking to me now?"

"Mr. Lake felt it was time that you specifically knew about him and his work." The cobra rose from its coil and took over speaking from the rhino. "He is a part of the UltraNet itself and has become aware of your research. Don't worry, he's not looking to penalize; he wants to equip you with knowledge in the hopes you can turn it into wisdom."

Niko belched and relived his hefty breakfast for several microseconds. He had taken so many precautions to conceal his path across the UltraNet and it's darker pockets. *A part of the UltraNet itself? What does that even mean?*

"Are you ok?" The rhino, Hammer apparently, asked with genuine concern.

"Yeah, yeah I'm ok. It's just that… I… How… *What is this day…*"

"It's Wednesday," the cobra, Sickle, responded.

"I know, that's, that's not what I meant," Niko shook his head and fixed his eyes on the pair of animals.

"Ok, I'll bite, what 'knowledge' does this Mr. Lake wish for me to have?"

"To put it simply Mr. Sanzenbacher, his origin story," Sickle responded.

"Mr. Lake feels," Hammer the rhino picked up the conversation. "That once *you* are aware of how he and his came to be and where we are all located, well, the perspective of your current mission will expand."

"My current mission," Niko parroted.

"Yes. You are transferring to London to be with that Drexler girl. She's special, been looking out for her for some years now."

Years?

"You are in good hands with her. But Mr. Lake insists that he be revealed to you at this exact juncture in time."

"Does *she* know about you two and this Mr. Lake?"

"In due time. However, she must not know until Mr. Lake feels it appropriate. His timetable is what counts now," Sickle rewound herself around the prominent main horn of Hammer's face.

Niko checked the time.

1215pm.

Niko turned around and saw the River People gorging on their enormous roasted fish. A Floating Pharm gently bobbed passed. The burgeoning, heaving, ship brought with it a flock of hummingbirds and a robust swarm of bees. He looked up at the sprawling bridge that connected two major walkways. Sunlight poured down like water from a fire sprinkler. The mist of warm illumination wafted onto his skin causing him to break into a gentle sweat. The green and blue light twerking on the water reminded him of Margeaux's eyes.

Margeaux.

Does she really *not know of this Mr. Lake?* Her scrunched up expression from when they departed made him smile.

A nearby sentient cluster of Kopou Phool began to emote, reminding him of Takanohana. Surely the massive bloom was thriving, given the effective display of protection several hours earlier. In the air above, messenger pigeons flittered to and from their respective destinations.

Niko let out a deep, long sigh and returned to looking at the cobra and rhinoceros. He cracked his knuckles and clapped his hands in a moderately anxious display.

"Ok, I guess I've got the time, so, shoot. Tell me of this mysterious Mr. Lake."

10

Project WISELAKE

My mouth was a stinging parched rot, Hammer, the rhino with a pink crystal horn, started.

I could feel each individual tooth pulse in its socket.

Mohinder told us over and over, beforehand, of how he merely modified some store-bought Sol Verde RABIOSO's by soaking them in a solution comprised of formaldehyde and liquid ketamine. I initially questioned his method of curing, leaving them to hang in a bandolier over his maple-syrup-driven hog-smoker (imported from L'Empire Glorieux du Québec), but, the sweet crispiness of the inhalate was an admittedly nice touch.

I received the third cigarillo of the night into my right hand. The wrap felt like sticky crystalized sandpaper. I did three repetitions of some old Japanese breathing exercises and enjoyed the rush of oxygen. I took a slow, fulfilling, drag and repeated the same muscular oscillations that accompanied the breathing exercises. I felt a tickle in the lower right corner of my left lung.

Astrid took the crayon-sized sugary stump from me and reminded me to exhale. She giggled her sweet giggle while I coughed and roiled.

The fire we had lit as a group had shifted to an alluring purple. I paid for the color enhancements and I was more than satisfied with the dazzling array thus far; although I will admit the things I was seeing may very well have been a part of the substances we had all ingested that evening.

I turned my attention from the octopus made of ferns and pomegranate seeds that had joined us and concentrated on Astrid's shins. Depilation had always bothered me, but the way the firelight was reflecting on her bare shins calmed me down. She made the choice to depilate so I had no other option but to respect her decision.

Hours passed.

During our time together around the fire, Astrid continually brought up Marx, Mao, and Stalin. At first, I was put off as Wednesday was our traditional day to discuss historical politics, but I soon found myself unable to think of anything other than the Bolsheviks, Julian October, suffixing 'grad' to place names, and a shade of red so entrancing I became lost in the infinity that came with it.

After what seemed like several hours worth of discussion on the effectiveness of implementing a democratic system of promotion in the workplace instead of a merit-based one, Astrid took my hand and led me away from the others. At a safe enough distance, she turned and told me of a rumor: near the chosen area of tripping, there exists a bit of Black Science.

Suddenly, she kissed me. Her lips were white-hot thorium and her tongue a radioactive serpentine.

Thus far, we had only held hands and exchanged a few pecks, but the thought of dabbling in banned applications of logic really seemed to get her motor running. Come to think of it, one time we went to the Museum of Experimentation and listened to a lecture on the dangers of illegal research. By the end of it, she was flushed, a little sweaty, and doing everything in her power to not ravage me; kisses still withheld. Her self-control was both legendary and enviable.

She giggled at the trail of saliva that tethered our faces as she pulled away from me. The most satisfied, yet appetizing, look drizzled down her face, starting at her bleary eyes.

"I hear it's just through these trees…" She took a firm grip on my hand again and blazed a trail away from the others and through the thick tropical foliage. With each encroaching step, the tenants of Mao Tse Dong's brand of Communism suddenly became very present in my mind. *Cultural Revolution…* I did my best to brush away the Red Hype, but the more I tried to not glorify the proletariat, the more propaganda I seemed to conjure. *The power is in the peasant…*

There was a temperature jump. We'd collided with a bulwark of humidity and swelter.

I could see sweat running down her neck. I loved it when she skipped deodorant, but I hadn't the stones to tell her so yet. Her natural scent was a powerful narcotic. I was already addicted and I hadn't even had a full hit.

A rhythmic humming sound began to bombard the Will Of The Workers growing in my head.

She walked straight into an invisible wall.

"Dawf…"

"Are you ok!?" I caught her on the rebound.

She rubbed her jutting nose and shook off the jolt. Her lips and philtrum throbbed and buzzed.

"This must be it…" She used the hand not clutching her nose to feel about the solidified air vallation we had discovered in the middle of the Ocala forest.

I chose to make no further comment on her running-into-the-wall as she had so readily moved on. A wave of euphoria washed over me. I felt a hearty, very specific type of satisfaction. While she searched for a way passed the invisible fortification, I followed, grinning, searching myself for the root of said satisfaction; a false memory of a full day's worth of factory work under the benevolent, in-person, gaze of Josef Stalin clotted in the middle of my mind.

We've never met Stalin, not even his Amplified clone… I forcefully told myself. But still I could not explain the realness of his face.

The more I thought about it, the clearer his face became.

I tripped on an exposed root.

My chin was bleeding. My teeth rang like Tibetan bells. The bush I fell into had a hard and unforgiving golden plate beneath it.

I gathered myself and took a good look at the plate itself. Again, I *knew* I had never seen it before, but I also knew, and with equal strength of clarity, what to do next.

I collected some of the blood from my chin and smeared it on the seal: an embossed hammer and sickle floating above a red five-point star, all encompassed by red and gold Cyrillic and Chinese writing.

The star lit up and gently pulsed. I next felt it pertinent to place my entire left hand over the seal, making sure the star nestled into my palm. The star grew hot, but I couldn't pull my hand away.

The rim started to glow.

Astrid looked on with a powerful confusion.

In a bizarre oozing motion, Little purple worms of electricity now emanated from the seal. They gathered themselves together like a crush of migrating caterpillars and lunged for the besmircher of Astrid's nose.

The wall shook and a doorway was cut open. Astrid, gape mouthed and gorgeous, groped for my hand. I joined my right hand to her left, and we slowly conducted ourselves beyond the maw.

The solidified air mass bounced the sound waves emitted by our breathing into an uncomfortable echo. Outside of our existential need for gas exchange, there were no sounds in the conduit.

We walked, with her taking the lead, until we could no longer feel the congealed air.

"Take your shoes off, please."

"This is it!" Astrid was instantly giddy.

"Who said that?" I asked out loud.

"I did, please, your shoes."

Not seeing any body connected to the voice that was directing us, I had no other choice but to remove my shoes. I helped Astrid take off her Japanese made UberShoes, and when I did, I noticed the neat little cubbies seemingly built just for our feet coverings.

When the shoes were neatly away, I stood and turned around to see nothing but darkness. Astrid took my hand once more and pulled me to her. She was ripe and I was in olfactory heaven.

"Hello, Comrades."

"Who's there?" I called into the void.

"There's no need for fear. We are all equals in this realm. No one is better than any one else. There are no classes."

"Can we, can we see you?" Astrid called out.

"Yes. I can tell you two are inclined towards Scarlet Sympathy."

The gap in the air sealed shut.

"Please, take three steps forward."

We did.

A peaked green light swelled up from a space below ground level. I looked down and tried to find the source, but only came to realize how humid the air was.

The smell was that of a very clean pool with little to no chlorine.

As the light increased in intensity, I could make out more shapes in the space. There were glass columns full of golden spheres and what could only be tendrils of hair. The orbs vibrated as the light swelled. The columns were arranged in triangular groups of three at the four cardinal directions. I was able to locate the source of the humming: a set of cute doll-sized computer consoles with no obvious wires or source of power. They were small, but they were active, and loud.

Then I saw him.

The lights were bombarding us with their lumens from their source in the bottom of a pond. After regaining myself, I noticed the body of water was the size and depth of a large professional wrestling ring. The golden orbs quivered with an increasing passion.

The green lights at full strength at last revealed our host. I tried, I really did, to accept what lived in the pool, but I just couldn't grasp the mechanics of 'how'.

In short, our host was a giant brain.

"I used to be a whole person," the brain began. "After the war I illegally entered China via New Tsarist Russia.

"I donned the garb of a Uighur and grew a beard. To avoid the DNA scans and The Party, I lived as vagrant; in those days, no cared who you were if you stank and slept in the street.

"I puttered around and did my best to lay low. Why did I break into the antipode, do you ask? I was looking for an old scientist friend of mine who had been recalled to Beijing, like most Chinese citizens, in the lead up to The War."

At this point, I looked for some chairs and found two where there none, not five minutes earlier. They were comfortable leather and glided across the grass with ease. I nestled myself into mine while Astrid draped herself across hers. I reached into my vest and withdrew a softpack of Sol Verde Blancos. I slid two stuffed cannabis and highly processed erythroxyl extract sticks out and lit them both. I passed one to Astrid and prepared for the brain to continue transmitting his story into our minds.

"I found Doctor Bao Guang Fang after 129 days of life as an illiterate wandering vagabond. Eating from the trash wasn't *so* bad, if I may say so. His lab was hidden in Taipingqiao, not far from Dongju.

"After we exchanged pleasantries on the street, he put on a bit of drama and made a scene of taking me in. This was done to present an image of benevolence and philanthropy to any onlookers, The Party included. Here was Dr. Fang, tearing himself away from his crucial and essential work to take in and care for a homeless Uighur, lost in the eternal, gem-like, capital. As we went in, I saw an old woman wipe a tear from her eye.

"Right away, Dr. Fang brought out a metal cigarette case and opened it. I stared at the plain white cylinders and remembered the feel of a nicotine flush."

"Just ordinary, plain, tobacco. Care for one?" The doctor flicked one into his mouth and extended the case in my direction. With a slight and turgid reluctance I reached out and accepted one of the sticks. His lighter had a test tube clutched by a foreboding spider. The smoke was crisp and the nicotine dizzying.

"So, how did you find me?" The doctor asked, with a deeply relaxed expression plastered on his round face.

"I did my best to explain the harrowing 129 days I had just experienced, but after ten minutes of rambling, I came to the realization that I had found him by pure chance.

"That morning, I woke in an old tennis court near Fuchengmenwai. For whatever reason, a sparrow landed on my shoulder, before taking off. I instantly found myself entranced by the small creature. I have no idea what was so bewitching, but I soon found myself stumbling about, mouth agape, trying to catch up with it. I ran, and ran, and felt no hunger or thirst. Time became a hot stick of butter over a raging fire. Before I knew it, I was in Taipingqiao. It was a beautiful day. There were people all about. I lost the little sparrow just outside the doctor's door."

"Dr. Fang chuckled at my tale. I took a few more drags on my cigarette and set it on a nearby uranium-glass ashtray. From this point on, Dr. Fang only wanted to talk about one thing: Project Wiselake.

"One night, while particularly sauced on snake whiskey and methaqualone, Dr. Fang was assaulted by an idea. His prospect was so enthralling, and the substances so lingering, he walked the streets of Beijing for fifteen hours straight, thinking, plotting, analyzing. When the compounds wore off he returned home to his lab and began a procedural assessment.

"He expressed a weighty gratitude for The Party's permission of what the UN had deemed illegal, Black Science. He then equally lamented the inability to house what would become of his idea within China proper, despite their leniency. This oxymoronic situation began to stir feelings of paranoia within me, but my history with the man himself reminded me that no matter what happened, no matter what decision I chose to make, I was in good hands.

"As he continued explaining the finer details, we relocated to a large western-style kitchen where the good doctor went to work preparing some food for the two of us. He talked while he cooked. His ability to be so bitingly scientific while making the most delicious Kansai omelet's I've ever had was uncanny. We ate and had several Chinese cigarettes and beers. The entire time he never once stopped talking.

"When he finally finished, after another meal

and round of beer cancer sticks, he asked what I thought of the whole enterprise. I took the paper towel Dr. Fang had provided as a napkin and dabbed my mouth. For a solid seventeen seconds I sat still and said nothing. Just as the doctor went to resume speaking, I cut him off and expressed my enthusiasm. After all, given the results of The War and my illegal immigration status in China, I felt I would be a perfect specimen.

"He cleared his throat along with the metal table we ate at and smiled at me."

"Walk this way," Dr. Fang intoned as he lead me down a narrow hallway to his workbench. The injections weren't *so* bad. Just two or three dozen pricks and I was out like a light. I dreamt of peasant uprisings and governance derived from homegrown socialized democracy. I saw a perfect melding of Mao and Marx with a tropical utopia as a result. I spent two summers with Lenin and Trotsky. Fidel Castro took me to the movies. Enver Hoxha and Josef Stalin helped me paint a fence. Deng Xiaoping showed me how to prepare a field for harvest. Edith Lagos taught me to shoot, Rosa Luxembourg and Nadezhada Krupskaya had me out for a picnic. At one point, I enrolled in an infinite university and came to a powerful understanding of robotics, ethics, agriculture, civics, horticulture, pharmacology, industrialization, and a wildly vast number of other fields.

"The dreams intensified. Walls of palpable color and visual sounds overtook me. Tastes and textures embarrassed my tongue. The aroma of a million roses drove me to some form of blindness, believe it or not. The dreams were so long and bewildering, I forgot they were no part of reality.

"When I next 'woke', I was as you see me now. Dr. Fang took care of everything. His father was a frightfully potent arm of The Party's governing body, so getting me out of China was as simple as throwing a rock over a fence. He said he picked Miami as it held the best soil for the second half of his idea. He set up the orbs and the cute regulating computer nearby. All of it runs on the ambient power I now produce. I also constructed and maintain the wall of air your Astrid ran into. Dr. Fang explained part of the intended results of his idea was extreme Amplification, and in my case, telekinesis became my arms, legs, and eyes.

"And here I am Mr. Lake. Emperor and Grand Nabob of The Robotic Caribbean Communist Coalition."

I noticed my mouth was hanging open. Astrid was equally astonished.

"Oh, I'm also the shadow coach of the Miami United Workers Party. I let Ineko Asanuma calls plays from time-to-time but for the most part it's all me. I watch the games via net-enabled periscope and SMS my will to Ineko."

Still, I remained incredulous. I mean, it was a

brain, a colossal one at that, and he is talking to me in my own mind, about how he is the one in charge of forty million humans and another ten million humanoid robots.

Given the circumstances, I had no other choice but to believe this experience was indeed *not* a hallucination.

Mr. Lake gave us time to let his background settle into our psyches.

"Ok, so, what of all this?" In a brief moment of crystalline lucidity I wondered why we were here and what his story had to do with us.

"I'd like to hire you two. Permanently," Mr. Lake transmitted his desire into us. "You will be remade into beings that can pass through the thin fabric of our shared reality. Whereas I can absorb any bit of information placed anywhere on the UltraNet, I cannot interface with anyone outside of this immediate vicinity. Were I to lower the solidified wall of air and project myself out, I would most certainly be found and eradicated in a grand display of 'ethical scientific reasoning'."

He did have a point.

"The Professors and Scientists that have claimed their spot on the brand new world stage have become aggressively religious with their ethics enforcement. As you already know, most liken the modern University system to a white-washed Spanish Inquisition."

"OK. I'll bite. How exactly would we be used to represent you outside of your sanctum here?" I asked Mr. Lake.

And here we are.

Mr. Lake improved upon methods developed by a Cartel Kingpin in Mexico to relocate our minds into these bodies. My horn is comprised of foundational elements of time and space, thus allowing me to slice open doorways to anywhere Mr. Lake needs us. Astrid, I mean Sickle, can project images and alter perceptions of anyone mentally feeble enough to work in the government.

Mr. Lake says that he is satisfied with what we've shared with you. As you continue on to London with the Drexler girl, he, and we, will never be too far off. Please safeguard this information, his identity et al, and only tell the Drexler girl when *you* feel it appropriate. If she really is sincere about her hate for Shopping, it will come out, and you may tell her everything. There have been others, and they were liars.

Take care Mr. Sanzenbacher.

11

The rhino with a pulsing pink gem of a horn and the black cobra coiled around it, Hammer and Sickle, retreated into the greenery. Niko shuffled backwards until a rock formation surprised him and became a sitting place.

More birds fluttered by.

More boats of differing shapes and sizes floated and motored past.

"*There were others, they were liars,*'" Niko said out loud. To no one. *Have I been fooled?* Niko ran over his interactions with Margeaux, 'the Drexler girl.' She was very much his brand of gorgeous. She didn't wear deodorant. She didn't shave *anything*. She was pale as marble and sharply featured with a big nose and long stringy yellowish-red hair. Her butt tear-dropped and poked out like an air conditioner. She was rabidly intelligent and could outthink any human he'd ever met. When she spoke, her S's were so sharp and crisp that dogs reacted with each cutting use of the nineteenth letter of the English alphabet. She was everything and more that Niko had ever desired.

Have I been fooled by her perceived greatness?

He had been before. A young woman had used Niko several years earlier to project an image of virginity. The entire ordeal involved Niko thinking he and she were to be wed as soon as possible. But after the umpteenth delay, he put aside his rosy glasses and investigated her dealings. She was lying. She was already married to a deadbeat recluse who breathed in her lies like cigarette smoke. Niko hadn't been back to Mumbai since.

But Margeaux was different. Her anger at the Shoppers was real. Her hatred of Clancy and the other Kings was palpable. Her kisses were... *No!* When her father was brought out on that stage and threatened with force-feeding , her horror was true, real.

Niko needed a walk.

He climbed up from the embankment and lugged his pack down the well-manicured road.

Just twenty-four more hours...

He walked a large circuit until it was dark. He was tired from carrying the pack around the city, so he dropped into an omnibus station and locked up his goods. From there he dropped into an automat and grabbed some Pad Thai, three mangosteens, some rose lemonade, and a Thai Coffee. When he had finished eating and people watching, a movie seemed perfect. As the film started, a dark comedy about two female rivals having to care for their drunk mutual enemy, Niko located his softpack and sparked up a Sol Verde Ojo de Oro orbital cigarette. Shaped like a bomba yerba mate gourd complete with a metal siphon, the Durban Poison cannabis, opium, and scorpion tail mélange made the movie a zombie rom-com. Although his laughter came at the right moments, the length and guttural nature put off more than a few of the other patrons.

Niko checked his watch when the film was over. *18 more hours...* He chose to head across town to the theater with couches, easy chairs, a full-service exotic hamburger bar, and no children allowed.

The trip through the panting downtown area was fraught with misunderstandings, thanks to the V² Sol Verde company of Mexico City.

Niko arrived in a sweat. It was not in any way hot, he was just paranoid after using the bathroom in a flower shop that openly advertised a lack thereof.

He slithered over to the burger bar and ordered the house specialty, the Trust Us Burger: two patties (comprised of nearly any meat you could think of. Niko chose a blend of Kobe Beef and Camel), grilled crimini mushrooms, cashew cheese, heirloom tomatoes, bacon, a fried egg, garlic aioli, house-made ketchup, and romaine lettuce, all served with melted butter on a toasted pretzel bun. He chose tempura-fried green beans and a liter of Indian lager to wash it all down.

Tonight the theater was having an all night Horrorfest. The first movie was Slash Through The Ashes, a brutal send-up of a Cricket rivalry taken a bit too far. Once more, Sol Verde altered the perception of this series of movies so much that Niko's screams of terror were converted to shrieks of laughter. The other patrons chose to indulge themselves via their own bags from LeRoy's as opposed to chiding him for his enjoyment.

The manager woke him at 0900am. His teeth felt like wearing thick parkas full of ants.

Niko creaked and popped until he was upright. The floor dipped and restabilized.

"Thanks," Niko said, his breath comprised of hot ash and remorse.

Ten more hours...

He set out for the road.

Niko elected to maintain a perimeter around his current Store so that he could walk in and receive his transfer the moment they opened.

He walked by a koi pond supply store and was reminded of Mr. Lake. Hammer's transfixing horn. Sickle's shiny scales. The smell of cotton candy after the pair had departed from him. On a holovision in a nearby bar, Niko saw a Polymatic Football Update. The Miami United Workers Party had traded one of their few human players, 2DE Oleg Murmansk, to the Estes Park Simulacra for 3CB DeForest Jenkins, a simulacrum. Niko initially reeled at the news. A simulacrum had never played for Miami, the team mainly comprised of humanoid robots sans falseflesh and a hypereal appearance; the average Miami player looked like something you'd find assembling cars in factory somewhere in Ford's Detroit Metropolis. The fans had come to accept the silver and black exposed metal that shown through the brilliant, but redundant, red-on-vermillion jerseys, with the exception of their human Quarterbacks, Leonid Kim and Sample Wong. Now with a simulacrum in the nickel, the defense would simply never look the same.

202

Niko gathered himself and envisioned Mr. Lake orchestrating the trade: The great and cumbersome mass of gray matter and the glass columns of hairy vines coiled around vibrating golden spheres telling Hammer and Sickle to make the call to Estes Park.

After the panel of two women, one man, and a retired simulacrum player discussed the trade and its ramifications, the channel moved on to the World League of Intoxicated Automobiling. Seven-time champion Slick Babtunde's 1944 Leyland Tiger careened across the finish line. Rudi Como was hot on his tail, but Babatunde clearly owned the Windhoek Circuit.

Niko always wanted to try out for the WLIA. Once, he drank a six-pack of Indian lager, took an MDMA capsule, and lined his dash with Sol Verde Sencillos. He rented a bright pink restored 1947 Packard Custom 8 and took it to a WLIA sanctioned practice track. The substances kicked in shortly after the third lap. Niko didn't wreck, but he didn't cross the finish line either. He passed out on lap eight, of 150. That experience gave Niko a healthy respect for the women and men that tanked up and got behind the wheel in a healthy environment designed specifically for sport. Plus, the healing plants and machines now extant made the injuries from any wreck as easy to repair as a flat tire.

Unable to control himself, Niko dashed into a sporting goods shop and impulse-bought a Rudi Como jersey. It was a lime green bowling shirt with a nametag on the upper left breast that read 'Rudi' in shining gold stitched cursive. On the back was a rosy and intensely bright pink number fourteen. The stitching was fine and sturdy. The jersey itself had a breathable plastic softness to it. The collar was pink, matching the shiny and radiant number. He worked the keys necessary free from his heavy key ring and paid. The clerk folded up his purchase, placed it into its soy-plastic bag, and slid the item across the clear plastic counter.

"Thank,"

"Thank," Niko replied.

Can't do that too many more times... he thought. Niko was getting increasingly paranoid as his hour of transfer drew near.

At 1400pm Niko decided to answer the call of his stomach. He got on the monorail and rode three stops to Scotch-Viet Town.

He sat down at a street café and a gorgeous red-haired Vietnamese woman in a tartan brought him a bowl of pho with Scotch Eggs and a side of chips. He watched life happen in the bustling boulevard that the café had barnacled onto. The center lane was strictly for the driverless omnibus. The next lane was taxis and rickshaws. The outer lanes were for privately owned vehicles. Next was the sidewalk, lined with trees and overflowing with people. Overhead the monorail silently delivered people to their stops. The sound of flowing water, that of the dual air-purifying rivers on the inside of either sidewalk —separating the bestirred masses from the road by three meters— made Niko relax. He ordered a large rose lemonade and carefully observed a group of teenagers in saris taking photos and laughing their way from shop to shop. Their happiness and effervescence refreshed him and for a brief second made him forget the world was having its strings pulled by a group of people who fancied themselves as elite Customers of one another.

The Customer's always right.

Niko paid and left the café. The waitress winked as he handed her the requisite number of keys.

For the next few hours Niko rode the monorail and tried to guess where different people were getting off. Some old men in turbans got off near the botanical gardens. An old blue-skinned woman dressed like a go-go dancer got off at the stop that doubled as an entrance to a sprawling grocery store. A mother and her two daughters headed for a library with obviously overdue books. Sometimes Niko would just stare at the landscape visible from his seat.

The land in Assam was alive and invigorating. The air was always sweet. The temperature was always perfect. He loved the hot rain and the fresh tea. His mind had become hardwired for Tea Garden time. Most of all, everything in Assam was so *clean*. The city administration opened the floodgates of technology and innovation in regards to civil cleanliness in lock step with the heavily enforced UN Sanitation Protocols.

It was during his twelfth lap of the city that he realized it was time.

Niko arrived at the green and gold door at 1900pm on the dot. He looked around, so as to make sure that he was, of course, alone, and proceeded to massage the raised 'CB' with his thumb. The routine action was reciprocated with an equally ingrained set of motions; the door silently popped open. He slid in and the door *clicked* shut. His first instinct was to head straight to the locker room and change into his uniform, but Margeaux said the transfer would be waiting upon arrival...

A bellhop in purple grabbed Niko's arm.

"Uh, y-yes?"

"Nikolaus Ito Sanzenbacher?"

"Yes,"

"Come with me."

Niko was taken through a series of winding hallways that all smelled like old produce. The pair walked and walked for an uncomfortable amount of time. The hallways all *looked* different, but the smell never changed. His shoes wouldn't stop squeaking. The bellhop never once looked back to check on Niko. A set of double doors came and went. Several single doors with little portholes in them also made brief appearances. Niko never saw another person, besides the purple bellhop.

After the 27th doorway, single or otherwise, the pair entered the Departure Apparatus. Abdul the purple bellhop, as his now-visible nametag indicated, handed the DoorMaster a shimmering golden ticket. He then leaned in and whispered something into the orange DoorMaster's ear and used a large thumb to indicate Niko. The people conversed for several seconds, nodded to each other, then Abdul tipped his hat to Niko, and left.

The woman in orange that was this store's DoorMaster waved Niko over and pointed him to Slot 47. Niko smiled and obeyed. He waited, alone, his toes on the white line, for his door to be conveyed over to him. He was alone at this moment due to the Shopping in this Store only having just begun. The space was large and there was a draft despite there being no visible windows or source of air. The floor was black, as was the vast empty space before him where the doors were conjured. Niko turned and looked back at the Laotian DoorMaster. She smiled and fed the golden ticket into her console. The output matched the input, so she summoned the door for the London Branch.

Presently, a circular door with a golden knob in the center emerged from the dark and docked at Niko's feet. He swallowed hard and gave another look at the DoorMaster. She smiled back and waved him off.

Niko grasped the smooth and cold knob, turned it, and entered.

After the feeling of being doused in ice cold leeches and boiling air left, Niko found himself in a very similar looking staging area. He looked to his left and saw a portly black DoorMaster clad in electric periwinkle.

"Hello, hello. You must be Mr. Sanzenbacher?" his accent indicated he had grown up in Nairobi.

"Yes, yes that's me."

"Ok then! Your ride is out front."

Niko made sure he still had his pack and made for the exit.

"Oh, Mr. Sanzenbacher?"

"Yes?"

"*Mr. Lake sends his regards*," the man said while making a strange expression.

"What?!"

"Huh? I didn't say anything," the round and smooth ebony man gave Niko a scrutinizing look. Suddenly, the man gave the air around him an aggressive sniff and changed subjects "Do you smell that?"

"Smell what?"

"It's like, like, a freshly cleaned Parisian Metro station. Or, like a really spicy Thai duck curry…"

"That's a pretty broad spectrum, if you don't mind my say so," Niko said while slowly creeping towards the exit tunnel.

"Yeah, I know, but I cannot seem to escape the miasma…" The man picked up a corded phone and called someone. "Hey, yeah, it's me, could you come down here and sniff the air? What? I know! Just come!" and he slammed down the receiver.

During the call, Niko made for the exit. This tunnel was short and sweet. He depressed the bar that opened the clunky door and emerged into a warm London rain on a dark night. He could make out a beckoning black cab with an open door just four or five meters ahead. A sign tacked onto a building across the road read 'Lewisham'.

Lightning cut across the sky, brightening the area for a brief second.

Immediately there was an umbrella over his head.

"Niko!"

"Margeaux?"

"A head? In a plastic bag? Really? And just who is this 'Mr. Lake' that keeps harassing me?"

She grabbed him by the arm and marched him into the cab. The driver was a bot, so Margeaux felt free to talk. She began poring over events that occurred during their separation.

She knew about Sachin.

She clearly knew about his former job as a no-questions-asked courier.

She knew how to orchestrate a trans-global relocation.

Who is she really?

The cab pulled off and merged with the other cars brave enough to come out in the torrential downpour.

Again she surprised him with a forceful and aggressive kiss. She tasted like clean rose and saffron

Turkish delight. Her hair smelled like a garden of confections. Her natural scent wafted through her shirt every now and then.

The cab continued through the maze of southern London.

After twenty minutes of mobility, the cab slowed and pulled into a driveway.

"We're here, 44 Breakspears. That's our address."

Our address?

Margeaux took the lead in making sure the pair made it safely indoors. When the door closed, Margeaux tapped away on her phone for several seconds.

Niko looked out of the window when he heard a strange noise and watched as the cab they arrived in dissolved into a puddle that the rain washed away.

"I'm not taking any chances," she said while hanging up her dripping jacket. She turned and clapped her hands, causing the holovision to turn on. Immediately the front room of the free-standing manor was flooded with the music and humanity that comprised Wednesday Night Football. The Mexico City V^2 Immortals were at home against the Saigon Amalgamated Clanship.

Another peel of lightning shook the borough.

The rain increased in frequency and palpability.

"So, Niko, welcome to London."

CUSTOMER BUTTCHEEKS

ORGANIZATIONAL STRUCTURE:

?
⇊
King
⇊
Viceroy/Master Chef
⇊
Executive Vice President
⇊
Regional Manager/Executive Chef
⇊
General Manager/Sous Chef
⇊
Shift Supervisor
⇊
Commis
⇊
Clerk III
⇊
Clerk II
⇊
Clerk I
⇊
Trainee

The following Bonus content has been brought to you by:

Traveling Carnival Rides, Amusements, Super Science, et al.

If you can think of it,
we can transmogrify it.®

BONUS TALE!

THE BALLAD OF RUDI COMO

The lines on the track were blurring.

Right on schedule.

The other drivers…

What other drivers?

I am the only extant driver.

The engine is making a bearded growl.

The instant I need them, my fingers are glow sticks.

I don't care.

The track is a vinyl record set to 1547 RPM beneath the rubber footpads of the living machine.

A semi-familiar knocking in my chest.

I had a heart once.

Then SHE took it.

On my lips the petals remain; Psilocybin grown in a modified fanged pitcher plant with a methylenedioxy-tinged fluid chamber.

Something else rests below my nose, aside from my mustache.

A burning stump of…

Nicotine? No.

The smoke feels too chunky.

I don't care what it is.

It's doing its job exceedingly well.

The track is curving now.

I turn the wheel to ensure the integrity of my adherence to the flow.

I am the only driver.

The lights and crowd noise…

Thank God that's over.

But they will be back all too soon.

My left foot is complacent.

In it's stocking, the congealing sweat and carbonated heat don't seem to faze it.

The right foot, however, the right foot is simply overwhelming in its eminence. Others doubt their self-worth in its presence without even realizing it.

The beast can roar because of this foot.

Trails have been blazed, mountains conquered, deserts trounced; truly this appendage has impacted an innumerable amount of people through the ages.

But I wouldn't know for sure.

I only guide the flow.

A very small corked jar of sand from a desert the other 95% of me has never been to sits on the dash, mocking the absence of my corporeal majority.

An inspiringly small sprouted redwood burl dangles from the rear-view.

Lab tests indicate a New Albionese origin. The time I've spent in New Albion included no trips to Mr. Muir's Woods, nor any other redwood vein.

Then there is the scar.

It still hurts sometimes.

The 12th Century, carbon dated, Mongolian arrowhead is now my necklace. The wound, being on the sole of my right foot, doesn't hurt *RIGHT NOW*.

And yet, when I am fulfilling my sworn duties as Commander-in-Chief, I become numb from the knee down. The pedal remains engaged. I, as Vehicular President, merely guide the flow.

There is only the flow.

I am the only driver.

100 Laps pass.

I need MORE.

The glove box is open.

I didn't open it.

Yes I did.

The flower buds crunch and the competition melts.

I am the only driver.

Another hundred laps.

Another quivering mouthful of lysergic flower buds.

The breeze clots and turns my hair into an anemone. Clown fish stream from the vents in the dashboard. I feel their gentle symbiosis in my follicles. My bench seat is the sea floor. Powerfully vermillion shrimp with electric rainbow accents are cleaning the area to my right.

The curve in the track changes nothing.

Finely tuned, 155 BPM, poly-rhythmic, drum kit destruction, awash in intricate cascades of eroding guitar, keeps my mind sharp and all the trains running on time.

Another hundred laps.

I yell in mistaken anger.

A miniature hive greets me from the glove box.

I am suddenly incredulous.

An engine revs, a horn blasts, and the words *"SIC SEMPER TYRANUS!"* climb into my machine through the roar; another driver is making an attempt at the Presidency.

I yank the Hive and its base from the compartment.

A second misguided outburst makes the Hive collide with the dashboard. A very large hornet is now liberated.

The eyes are what get me.

IT KNOWS HOW TO HATE ME.

Out of all other options, I laugh.

The stinger breaks the skin on the right rear of my jaw. Having embossed his seal, the yellow fiend expires.

I skipped the funeral.

My head is now a bullfrog's. I can see the bulbous lower lip in the rearview. Despite the weight, I can still breathe and harass.

A gate opens and the track morphs.

I am now overlord of the Common Man's road.

What I assume to be onlookers bray at me at nearly every turn.

My face is on their T-shirts.

WHY?

OH YEAH…

A sign says the flow has taken me down a street called 'Post'.

Saying the word out loud makes my teeth crisp; I feel a definite finality in the sharp cut that the finishing 'st' provides.

My term in office enters the Lame Duck phase.

Where the track was once dark absence, it now lay illumine. A cavalcade of refracted light establishes a route to the finish line.

In the side mirrors, only a paltry reflection of sport. The false Wilkes Booth has been neutralized.

The home stretch.

The apiary venom intensifies.

The right foot is waning.
The earliest traces of ant appendages are felt.
A turn.
A second turn.
An incline.
A hairpin-turn exercise around Union Square.
A long, drifting, third turn onto Kearney.

The machinery creating the flow that I merely guide continues functioning unabated.

The dead hornet tumbles and rattles in the eternally empty passenger foot well.

The swollen double-bass drum solo creating an avalanche from the shamelessly obese sub-woofers bolsters my bravado.

The final eleven blocks before the Broadway ascent.

My lower lip claps against the wheel.

I can feel a plasmatic heat around my eyes.

Synapse and tire rotation are superbly balanced.

Brown creatures, perhaps made of clay, pour from the vents. Their red eyes seek to condemn, but I refuse.

SHOCK!

Where did HE come from!?

Another driver beckons.

HOW DARE HE!

I reach to my stalwart glove box. A fistful of erythroxyl-phlox. My teeth grind the grass and unfeeling coats the maw.

More prickling agony from the right foot.

NOT YET!

My eyes claim that the person attempting to infringe on my right to the office of Commander-In-Chief is none other than Omar 'Slick' Babatunde. The sweating leather-bag-of-a-man's bulbous cantaloupe foot was causing immeasurable suffering to the gas pedal.

Slick Babatunde's sparkling green and black 1944 Leyland Tiger bus drops its gauntlet with a cyclopean sneer.

I accept the challenge and express my equally strong demand for satisfaction.

I deploy my emergency thermos. The hot and lumpy mixture of amphetamines and psychoactives goes down like a cup of hot mice.

At last, the flow is made manifest.

Searing pain.

My right foot is bleeding.

Sharp, burning agitation burrows its way into my calcaneus.

CAN SLICK SEE THE FLOW?

His cracked crimson eyeballs and drooling orifice indicate a solid perhaps.

He honks his horn.

Wait, maybe he didn't.

I HONKED!

With reckless impunity.

The passengers riding with Slick begin to accost me. This is odd as I was present for when Slick had the seats of the once beautiful bus torn out, and large engines put in. Their words don't make sense.

Just then, the degree to which Slick is simply stuffed into the driver's cab, overtakes me. I am struck by the absence of free space in his cab. All nine of his cocoa-colored chins are mere nanometers from the wheel. I'm not sure if he knows, but there are two bloated puffer fish trying to pass as his eyes. The coral reef and accompanying ocean has sloughed off of my existence and settled onto Slick's bus, displacing the babbling 'passengers.'

The flow shudders, signifying the end as nigh.

My once elegant leather shoe, with its buckle so satisfyingly polished, is now corpulent with plasma. The burrowing pain has stopped, but the burning weight remains.

With the end so close, I must jettison all distracting interest in the oceanography taking over the attempted juggernaut that is Slick Babatunde.

He inches closer.

I reject his advance with prejudice.

HE CANNOT HAVE MY VICTORY.

I reject the fine I have just incurred for bumping his vehicle.

I MERELY ABIDE BY THE FLOW.

I reject the usurper as a whole.

I AM THE COMMANDER-IN-CHIEF.

Our bumpers collide and form a shaky alliance.

I lose my demeanor and lash out; my firm, outlandish, repudiation of their coming together only adds to whatever Slick is experiencing.

My right foot lurches from the accelerator and clamps onto the brake. I spin the wheel to the east and send myself across the Victory line.

Slick is beside himself.

Seeing two of him makes me sick to my stomach.

A force extricates me from the controls.

I am floating on a sea of my people.

Camera flashes.

A kotinos slithers onto my head.

Now, I stand erect on a stage.

A portly trophy is presented, and I reassure it with a kiss.

Darkness is a lead blanket.

I can only feel my smile.

The crew chief appears.

Congrats.

The blanket is so warm.

The screen wipes.
Graphics fill the viewing area.
Remixed Gangsta-Swing-Step blares.
The show begins.

"What a finish! Typically the Stoned Reaper finishes all alone, but Babatunde would not go down quietly," Magnus Leuwenhoek opened the trailing live broadcast of the UN Global Sports Network's coverage of the World League of Intoxicated Automobiling. His blonde pompadour was famous, and his cohost made it visibly evident that she hated it.

Footage rolled of Rudi Como's 1961 Eureka Landau, drenched in the glossiest black paint with neon green flame accents, drifting sideways across the finish line. The bumper had temporarily entangled itself with Slick Babatunde's, reminding most of two stags caught alongside each other in the forest.

"I'd like to start by thanking the city of San Francisco for allowing the race and its unusual format," Rosalina Montevideo gave a close-lipped smile and nod. Her large, sharp, nose drew ones eye, but her own apertures never failed to fight back.

"Yes after the lap portion, things really heated up in the Rally-style finish, right Rosalina?"

"Psh, we watched the race together!" She said with a stout look of disgust for her longtime TV partner. *I hate his hair!*

"...Yes, we certainly did," Magnus cleared his throat. "Continuing our coverage of Rudi Como's record setting 14th straight win, why don't we take a look at his approved Schedule of Ingestments:

- **ERYTHROXYLUM COCA**
- **TRIMETHOXYPHENETHYLAMINE**
- **LYSERGIC ACID DIETHYLAMIDE**
- **METHYLENEDIOXYMETHAMPHETAMINE**
- **CAFFEINE**
- **NICOTINE**
- **TETRAHYDROCANNABINOL**
- **ET AL.**

"Oh my Rosalina, did you notice the 'Et al' at the end of his list?"

"I certainly did," she said as she stiffly fought his pallid gaze. Her long straight black hair poured over her shoulders and back like a mute waterfall. Wide-eyed and revolted, she smoothly continued, "I was not aware he had earned the privilege to mix in binding agents and flavor modifiers that may or may not improve cooperation of substances."

"Truly his doctorate has proven to be a boon in regards to his success in the WLIA."

"What about the other drivers?" Rosalina sighed, reassured herself, and made the slightest facial rejection of everything that Magnus stood for.

"...Chet Fescue wrecked at the onset of the rally portion..." Magnus continued his broadcast.

In the attic of his awareness, Magnus had placed in a readily accessible steamer trunk his concern regarding a recent attempt at pitching woo. The trunk's contents would tell a story of flowers and a beaming white chocolate and edible diamond-dust corset sent to the new lead MASSBALL* anchor, Orchid Nkemdiche. She was tall, dark, and Namibian; Magnus' desire made manifest.

Rosalina, though, was a bit of a hater. She simply could not stand interoffice romance after her falling out with a Key Grip and his Best Boy...

"...He was pulled, using the Jaws of Life, from his mangled red 1997 Ford Taurus."

The clip rolled.

"Oh... That looked pretty bad..." Her shock was genuine.

"That it did Rosalina. But I do believe the dislocated thumbs up he gave as he was loaded into the ambulance did inspire a modicum of hope in his fans."

Another clip, this time of crying Fescue Freaks, as they are commonly known.

"'Dirty Rita' MacFarlane was really the only other driver that may have at any time threatened Rudi's lead," Magnus sucked something out of his tooth and winked as the camera cut away to corroborate his testimony. "During the lap portion, they were neck and neck for a solid 200 rounds. When the gates opened and the Rally began though, from the film it looks like she was trying to light a tobacco

*Massachusetts Rules Pro Baseball

product, filthy habit, when she wrapped her 1976 Chevrolet Nova around that poor, poor oak tree."

"Yeah!" Rosalina stormed into the broadcast. "Pending toxicology, she could be liable for a Botanical Desecration fine. Here's what she had to say:

'I came 'round the firsht hairpin and, outta habit, I tried ta light my tradishnal Rally 'bacco when that fnuggin' shree juss came outta nowhere...'

"She looked pretty baked in that interview, Magnus."

"That she did Rosalina. How far the mighty have fallen, eh?"

"Man, I remember when she had that five-race streak only two years ago!" Rosalina's eyes bulged with reminiscence.

"I think it's her legendary 'Rally 'bacco'... filthy, awful stuff," Magnus screwed up his face in revulsion.

"Tell me about it!" *Milquetoast!* "Next week, we'll be calling the race from Olde England," Rosalina pivoted to camera B. "Do you think Rudi will be able maintain his renowned balance of focus and intoxication long enough to defend his title for a record-setting 14th straight win? What about Slick Babatunde?"

"He came pretty close today Rosalina," the blonde, fizzy-eyed, sportscaster continued bearing his hulking teeth.

"...Uh oh, breaking news folks, the living legend, the Stoned Reaper himself, Rudi Como, has already been listed as Probable for next week, pending a... *What did you say Jerry?* An emergency surgery to remove a *musket ball?*" Incredulity reigned on the set. "Yes… Ok… Folks they're telling me in my ear that I indeed read that bulletin correctly. Somehow, someway, Rudi Como managed to get a *musket ball* of some kind lodged in his foot *during* the race… make of that what you will." Magnus rolled his geodesic eyeballs in obvious disbelief.

"Y'know Magnus," *Lecher!* "The UltraNet has a bevy of theories regarding Mr. Como…" Rosalina was an avid poster across several so-called "lunatic fringe" message boards. Besides this, she was also an extremely high-ranking member of the infamously paranoid and destructive fan club, Como's Clones.

"Don't start with that again, it just doesn't make any sense. C'mon, the man is a star in a league *centered* on operating an automobile *while intoxicated*. I take a lethally-sized grain of salt along with *whatever* these racing professionals say."

"…All right Magnus. Whatever helps *you* get to sleep at night…" Rosalina regarded her co-anchor in the same manner one would while engaging a child who just swore belief in the gestational abilities of Mary Toft.

"Up next, we turn our attention to the endless and all-consuming world of PolyMatic Football…"

STAY TUNED FOR EPISODE 8, ACT II:

RIVALRY WEEK!

LPF Week 10

	V	
LA	V	SF
ROME	V	OTTAWA
DC	V	MOSCOW
MEXICO	V	TASHKENT
BANGKOK	V	SAIGON
ASSAM	V	MUMBAI
CHICAGO	V	NEW YORK
LONDON	V	PARIS
MIAMI	V	ESTES
UN	V	INCA
MUNICH	V	EDO (TOKYO)
CAIRO	V	SYDNEY